"You haven't won,"

Lindsey muttered against his sweater. "I know that's what you were thinking."

Jeremy laughed into her ear, his breath warm. "That isn't what I was thinking. Would you like to know what I was thinking?"

She nodded dreamily.

"I was thinking, if you can't get her drunk, Jeremy, old boy, you can at least get her tired." His right hand began a gentle massage from hip to shoulder. "You are tired, aren't you, Lindsey? Tired and thin and brave and tough and angry and—" she felt his lips graze her temple "—beautiful. So beautiful." He held her to him when she would have pulled away. "Relax, Lindsey. Forget my name is Boulanger, just for a little while. Enjoy yourself. You deserve it."

Surprisingly, she wanted to do just that. She was tired of fighting, tired of being alone, and it felt wonderful being held so securely, even if the arms surrounding her belonged to the enemy. Only he didn't feel like the enemy—not anymore.

Dear Reader,

Welcome to Silhouette Romance—experience the magic of the wonderful world where two people fall in love. Meet heroines who will make you cheer for their happiness, and heroes (be they the boys next door or handsome, mysterious strangers) who will win your heart. Silhouette Romances reflect the magic of love—sweeping you away with books that will make you laugh and cry, heartwarming, poignant stories that will move you time and time again.

In the next few months, we're publishing romances by many of your all-time favorite authors such as Diana Palmer, Brittany Young, Annette Broadrick and many others. Your response to these and other authors in Silhouette Romance has served as a touchstone for us, and we're pleased to bring you more books with Silhouette's distinctive medley of charm, wit and—above all—*romance*.

During 1991, we have many special events planned. Don't miss our WRITTEN IN THE STARS series. Each month in 1991, we're proud to present readers with a book that focuses on the hero—and his astrological sign.

I hope you'll enjoy this book and all of the stories to come. Come home to romance—Silhouette Romance—for always!

Sincerely,

Tara Gavin
Senior Editor

ELIZABETH KRUEGER

A Saving Grace

Silhouette ❤ *Romance*

Published by Silhouette Books New York

America's Publisher of Contemporary Romance

SILHOUETTE BOOKS
300 E. 42nd St., New York, N.Y. 10017

A SAVING GRACE

ISBN: 0-373-08774-8

First Silhouette Books printing February 1991

Printed in the U.S.A.

ELIZABETH KRUEGER

is the very first Silhouette author, to our knowledge, ever to have raised twelve children *and* developed her writing style to perfection. Perhaps her creativity has been inspired by the twelve lives she has guided and loved, or maybe her writing was her one escape from a household which at times must be impossibly chaotic. All we can be sure of is that we, her readers, are her true beneficiaries.

A Chicago native, Elizabeth now lives in northern Michigan. In *A SAVING GRACE,* her first romance novel, she has drawn on both locales.

NORTHERN MIDWEST STATES

Prologue

John Boulanger had told no one he was dying, not even his only child, Jeremy, who now sat across the large mahogany desk from him. His son exuded an air of negligent superiority which he wore as comfortably as an old suit of clothes and which, John knew, hid so very much. And, if it could be avoided, John would not mention his impending demise even now, although death was the only thing that had really frightened him in his sixty-odd years. Even so, he told himself, it did not scare him so much, this knowing in advance that his time was about up. It was just that he was never sure that his life would be truly over, or if the religionists were right and he would continue on some other plane. So, since fate had decreed that he would be given the opportunity, in death as in life, John Boulanger hedged his bets and protected his back. He had arranged everything methodically, precisely, with the tight control that had characterized the last fifteen years of his life. And now Jeremy must play his part, unknowing of the greater stakes.

"Scotch on the rocks?" John offered his son, then rose to walk softly across the plush deep brown carpeting to the gleaming wet bar that was part of his executive suite.

"You think I'm going to need it during this discussion?" Jeremy queried, gently probing.

"Maybe—" John kept his voice noncommittal, "—and maybe I'm just being hospitable to my only offspring, whom I have not seen for six months." His tone was bland, but there was enough accusation in his words to put Jeremy momentarily on the defensive.

After pouring a drink for Jeremy and one for himself, John turned and walked to where Jeremy was seated. "Here's your drink . . . son." Jeremy's dark eyebrows rose sardonically, and John damned himself for the sentimentality that caused his voice to sound hesitant, unsure. He stepped back so that he stood behind the expensive wing chair that Jeremy was using. He let his free hand drop to the chair back, momentarily touching the royal blue leather, which was also touching his son. John's hand rested there, brown and strong, the hand of a younger man, a healthier man. But he was neither, and he longed to use that hand to touch, to embrace, his son. The hand clenched involuntarily, and John withdrew it, moving to sit in his own chair behind his desk, deliberately swiveling it so that he turned from Jeremy to gaze out the wall of windows to his right.

Chicago was twenty stories below, but it was Lake Michigan, several city blocks away, that caught his attention. He had picked this office for its view of the lake, and the lake occupied his sight now. The skies were cold and angry today, and the lake was sending gray and white foam crashing over the rocks that composed the shoreline here. Clouds, heavy with the threat of a February snowstorm, hung low over the city, dimming the light of the sun. In the shadowed light the beehive of automobiles and people, also visible through his window, seemed far away and insignificant.

John's sharp, ever-active mind registered this, all the while acutely aware of the waiting stillness of his son.

Jeremy.

He was sorry for this strangeness between them now, even as he recognized the futility of attempting a change in their relationship after so many years. He was not sure he was capable of change himself, even though the desire, the need to say just once, "I'm proud of you, son," was so strong it caused an ache in his throat and a pain in his heart. Steeling himself, John turned to Jeremy. His face devoid of any emotion, his voice expressionless, he asked, "You do remember Ruth Ann Wellington?"

Jeremy's mouth tightened imperceptibly. "Of course."

The older man smothered a wry grin. *Like father, like son.* Jeremy gave nothing away, either. John's eyes flicked over the younger man's face, so very much like his own. The wavy black hair could have been his before it had turned silver years ago. The square, dominant chin was close to an exact replica of his own. The heavy eyebrows, the prominent cheekbones, all reflected Jeremy's paternity. Only the blue-black eyes were different, a gift from Marta, the one reminder of their short, painful marriage. There were, of course, other differences—Jeremy was taller than his father, and with twenty-five years between them, he was leaner, too. And he had about him an air of untamed maleness, which no amount of hand-tailored clothing could disguise. It was the kind of aggressive masculinity that only a woman's touch could soften. It gave John some pleasure that no woman had yet tamed his son, even though plenty had tried. It gave his plan some hope.

"Several months ago I traced Ruth Ann's daughter, Lindsey," John said calmly.

"Oh?" Jeremy said. Then, "Why?"

It was a fair question, and deserved a fair answer, if not exactly a complete one. He had to be absolutely convincing now, so that Jeremy would have no hint of any hidden agenda. John took a slow, easy breath. "I tried to keep in touch with Ruth Ann's daughter years ago, when...well, you know what happened. She would have nothing to do with me then, and I resolved to leave her alone, as that was so obviously what she wanted. But, I confess, it's nagged at me over the years—what happened to her." He paused, giving Jeremy time to fill in the gaps, to remember.

Jeremy's eyes met his father's stare evenly, giving no sign of the memories that were settling like distasteful medicine, sliding heavy and thick into his stomach. Fifteen years ago, Jeremy had been on the edge of uncertain manhood. His beautiful, faithless mother had long since disappeared from his life. But his father, who had seemed practically unaware of his existence, gradually began to take pleasure in "doing the town" with the shy, pleasing young man that Jeremy had become. A new, tenuous link of friendship and affection had been forged between them.

Then John Boulanger fell in love.

The recipient of John's overwhelming passion was, unfortunately, already married. That fact didn't stop John Boulanger, of course, and it wasn't long before Ruth Ann Wellington had abandoned her child and husband to join Jeremy's father. Divorce proceedings had been long and messy, but in the end, brash John Boulanger got what he wanted.

Having obtained his victory, Jeremy's father had swept Ruth Ann off to a wild, extravagant honeymoon in Las Vegas. There, John, feeling young and invincible, intoxicated with life and happiness, had done the one, stupidly careless thing that had cost him everything.

Jeremy had heard the news, along with the rest of the country, from a television set. Handsome, arrogant, self-made millionaire John Boulanger, while "driving under the influence," had run a red light in the middle of the Vegas strip. His car had been broadsided. His wife of only a few days had been killed instantly. John, however, had escaped with only slight bruises and a deep cut above his left eye, the scar from which he would carry all his life.

Consumed by grief and guilt, John Boulanger buried himself in his vastly successful business enterprises, earning a reputation for being coldly aloof from the rest of mankind. In the process of losing himself in profit and loss statements, John Boulanger forgot about his other link with humanity—his son. By the time he remembered, Jeremy had become his own man, and the fragile, wonderful, affectionate bond between them had been broken forever.

"Ruth Ann's daughter is in trouble, Jeremy." John's quiet words interrupted the younger man's uncomfortable flow of thoughts.

"What kind of trouble?" Jeremy asked, his mouth a thin, grim line of resistance, leaving unspoken the other question: *and what does all this have to do with me?*

John reverted to the businesslike tone with which he felt comfortable. "The detective I hired was thorough. I have here a complete report that I would like you to review."

"Why?" Jeremy asked for the second time, his tone short, arrogant, cold.

"Because you are going to see her, on my behalf," John explained softly, his eyes never wavering from his son's face. "You are going to persuade her to accept Boulanger aid. And you are going to bring her here, to me."

"You've got to be kidding," Jeremy said in a voice that was low and only slightly aggressive. "You know the schedule I'm keeping. Besides..." He shrugged and let the implication hang. The time was long past that John could give orders to his son and expect instant obedience. Both he and his father knew it.

"Jeremy," John paused thoughtfully, choosing his words with care, "it shouldn't be too hard for you to get away for a few days."

Jeremy regarded his father incredulously, as if believing for the first time that his request was serious. "Why don't you go see the girl yourself? After all, it's your debt," he stated callously.

A dull flush crept up John's face. Behind the desk his hands clenched as he felt the hotness of his face giving him away. "Yes," he bit out. "It is my debt. But she won't see me. The girl still refuses to have anything to do with me. I've tried. I've called. I've sent letters, I even sent money."

"That, at least, got a response, I'm sure," Jeremy muttered sarcastically.

"I received this yesterday." John handed an envelope to his son.

Jeremy opened it, then gave a shout of laughter. Inside the envelope was a check for $50,000, with a huge *NO* scrawled over it with a black marker.

"That's it?" he asked. "No letter or anything?"

"That's it," John said.

"It would almost be worth it," Jeremy said, his mouth twitching, "to meet someone who can't be bought with Boulanger money." Then his expression sobered again. "But I can't. I'm on the verge of getting Bill Abbott's account, after five years of waiting."

"Jeremy," John said softly, his eyes on Jeremy's face. "Damn Bill Abbott. This can't wait."

Jeremy shifted uncomfortably. "There are other considerations."

"In the guise of Lucille Abbott?" John issued the question like a challenge.

Jeremy looked away. "Perhaps."

"Are you serious about her, Jeremy?"

Again Jeremy was short. "Perhaps."

"But you're not in love with her. Maybe you like the idea that she's such a socially acceptable WASP, and you like it that her father is Bill Abbott, but you're not in love with Lucille."

Jeremy shot his father a look of ripping anger. "How the hell would you know anything about it?" he ground out.

John gave an almost indiscernible shrug. Then his voice grew low. "How important did you say the Abbott deal is to you, Jeremy?"

Jeremy understood immediately what his father was getting at. With terrible effort, he held his body rigidly still, his face carefully empty, while he waited for his raging anger to subside.

"Bill Abbott and I are old friends, Jeremy," his father reflected. "He owes me plenty of favors. One phone call from me and your deal with him is on . . . or off."

Jeremy's blue-black eyes flashed fire even as he rose out of his chair. "You would do that? You would interfere with my life in that way?" His voice was low, hard.

"I'm sorry, Jeremy, really I am. It's none of my damn business how your Abbott deal turns out, and I really don't care. But I want you to go see Lindsey, and I'll use any leverage I have to."

Jeremy looked at his father, stunned disbelief registering in his eyes before they turned as cold as ice. "No," said Jeremy. "No. As you said, damn Bill Abbott. And damn Lucille. And damn my whole business. I won't dance to your Looney Tunes because of threats, implied or real."

With barely controlled violence, Jeremy turned to leave, walking with savage footsteps to the door.

At that moment, John knew he had miscalculated with terrifying completeness. Jeremy was not bluffing. He had no lever strong enough. The whole game was over before it had begun. His mind racing, he came to an immediate, if distasteful, decision. "Jeremy." Again he made his voice low, trying to keep the old arrogance out of it, almost succeeding.

Jeremy's hand stopped on the doorknob, his back rigid.

"Jeremy, turn around, please." How it hurt to ask.

Slowly, with great deliberation, Jeremy turned, one brow raised in mocking response as he looked at his father.

"Jeremy, forget what I said, I should never have done it. I'm a rotten bastard, that goes without saying. But Jeremy, go see Lindsey, *please.*"

"Why?" he lashed out, curt and angry, demanding the real truth, acknowledging that the son knew the father had not been completely honest.

It was all John could do not to visibly slump in his chair. Instead, he stood slowly, even as he felt the energy draining out of him, as he was forced to admit both his physical weakness and his tactical error. He lifted his gaze, defeated but proud, to meet Jeremy's brilliant stare. "I'm dying of cancer, Jeremy. Dr. Mackel says six months, a year maybe."

Jeremy's face again went completely expressionless. John continued to eye his son, gambling everything on this last card. "I want to make my peace with Lindsey Wiltse, but she won't see me."

"Wiltse?"

"She's a widow with two children, and she's in real trouble. It's all in her dossier."

Determined brown eyes locked with fierce blue ones. Then Jeremy sighed, and with the sigh came a change, a minute softening. "My own father," he said wearily. "Why couldn't you just tell me you were dying? Why all the subterfuge and power play and manipulation? I'm your son, not your enemy."

Something approaching pure anguish flickered in the depths of John's brown eyes. He turned away. "Forget it, Jeremy. It was a bad idea, from start to finish. It's not important. Sorry to have taken your time this way." He sat down, picked up some papers on his desk, thus dismissing Jeremy without looking at him again.

"Damn you," Jeremy bit out grimly. "Damn you. You *are* a bastard. But you're also my father. Give me what you have on Ruth Ann's daughter. I'll go see her, when and if I can fit it into my schedule. But don't hold your breath. I doubt anything I can say or do will make any difference to the girl."

With one fluid motion, John set aside the papers he had been shuffling, picked up a thin folder that had been resting on the side of his desk, and held it out to Jeremy. Jeremy looked at his father one last time, resentment blazing in his eyes. Without a word he stepped forward and accepted the dossier, then turned and walked out of John Boulanger's office.

The economy of motion with which he moved did not hide the cold fury he felt, and it was only as Jeremy closed the door behind him with a deceptively quiet click that his father began to relax. An expression of infinite weariness filled John Boulanger's face, and hidden in the privacy of his office, he rested his head on his arms. After a moment he opened his top desk drawer to pull out an old picture of a young woman, auburn-haired, smooth-cheeked, the laughter of life seeming to dance in her eyes. "Ruth Ann," John whispered, intense longing in his voice. He leaned back in his chair. "A little bit tougher than I expected, Ruth Ann, but the game is in motion."

Suddenly he threw back his head and laughed, a bitter, barking laugh, and the sound held the echo of both victory and despair.

Chapter One

It was a good thing it was a slow night at the Northern Lights Donut Shop, the twenty-four hour sugar and caffeine stop that gave Lindsey Wiltse part-time evening employment. She stood behind the counter, scrubbing the white Formica with an energy that belied the exhaustion she felt. And with every scrub of the rag, she thought of John Boulanger. She wished with all her heart that she could wash away the effects of his most recent communication.

Fifty thousand dollars. John Boulanger had no right to do that, to tempt her in that way. By now he would have received her answer, and he would know that she would not allow him to buy off his guilt, no matter how badly she needed the money. She only hoped that the check meant he had a conscience, and that he was suffering now as a result of it. *Good*, she raged inwardly. He deserves every pang of remorse he might be feeling. Then, disgusted, she cursed herself for being a fool.

She moved down the short counter, scouring blindly at a spot left there by someone's coffee. Visions of her bed filled her with a longing so intense she felt her body must surely collapse on the spot. It would be nearly one before she could lay her head on her pillow, and less than six hours later she would be up to get her children ready for school and day-care, and she herself would be off to her daytime job as the administrative assistant to the owner of a local advertising agency.

Lindsey sighed deeply. Her replacement, Karen Black, was arriving at midnight, now only fifteen minutes away. Lindsey had never felt the time pass so slowly. It was probably due to her extreme fatigue. She felt tired, drained, and so fragile. Extremely fragile, that's me, Lindsey thought with a ghost of a smile. Handle with care. If only it were possible to rest for a while, a long while, and be at peace.

Thank goodness this was the slowest time of the night. At least she had no customers to serve.

As if on cue, Lindsey heard the bell tinkle above the door that admitted the public to the small shop. She looked up dazedly, force of habit putting a travesty of a smile on her pinched face as she raised her eyes to this unexpected patron. It was only after several seconds that her dulled senses took in the features of the man who towered over her five foot seven inch frame. Her eyes darkened in shocked recognition, causing them to look huge and wounded in her pale face. The floor seemed to rock beneath her feet, so that her fingers were forced to grip the counter where she was standing. While her mind screamed a rejection of what she was seeing, her body, already stretched beyond its normal limitations, swayed slightly.

"Is something the matter?" the tall man asked Lindsey, his voice even and expressionless.

"No...no, of course not." Lindsey's breathless voice sounded thin and defensive, even to herself. But he looked so much like John Boulanger, she thought she might have conjured him up, might be hallucinating his image. This was the face she had known and hated so many years ago, and was still trying to forget, to reject. But the eyes were different, electric blue-black in that dark face.

Lindsey's face had gone impossibly white, her own eyes reflecting her stunned confusion as she stared at the man intently. He was too young, she thought distractedly. He was too young to be the same man. But the likeness was great. Most likely he had been sent . . . she knew he had been sent. Desperately, she tried to gather her strength.

"You look like you have seen a ghost," the man stated in a sharp voice, his piercing eyes assessing her steadily. She thought she had never heard a voice so cold, or so cruel. She took a deep breath.

"Hi, Lindsey, I'm here." Relief washed over Lindsey when she heard Karen Black's breezy greeting. The other girl walked out of the storeroom, where she had used the back door to gain entrance. Karen was cheerfully tying on a spotless white apron, her blond hair swinging freely over her shoulders.

"Karen, take this one, please. I'm beat," Lindsey requested tautly. She did not care that she sounded abrupt, nor did she acknowledge the raised eyebrow on that oddly familiar face.

"Sure, hon, you go on home and get some rest," Karen replied easily. "Lord knows you deserve it." Lindsey turned to remove her own apron, then slipped into her winter coat. Out of the corner of her eye she saw Karen's expression melt appealingly as she turned to the hard-eyed man standing at the counter. "Can I help you, sir?" Karen asked, her voice husky in invitation.

He made no response.

Lindsey drew on her boots with quick, jerky movements, all the while feeling those cold eyes on her as a physical touch. She hoped her trembling was not obvious. If only she were not so tired, she would be able to handle this man's unexpected appearance with the casualness it deserved.

And she knew what those masculine eyes were seeing: a face devoid of any makeup, dull hair pulled carelessly away from her face by childish barrettes.

Of course he had been sent, she told herself again, and he couldn't have arrived at a moment of greater weakness to herself. She wondered who he really was. A duplication of those hated features could only be produced in a very close relative. Son? Nephew? Not likely a nephew. Son, then.

She stiffened her back and lifted her chin in a totally unconscious gesture, even as she remembered with a sinking heart that her ancient Ford station wagon was parked in front, which meant she would have to walk by the man in order to reach it. Lindsey considered using the back door and walking around the shop to her car, but her pride made her wince at such obviousness.

She hesitated only a fraction of a second. Keeping her chin high, her whole body a study of defiance, she moved quickly to the front door of the shop, deliberately not looking at the broad-shouldered man who stood there watching her. She felt him move beside her, and when she got to the door, she found he was already opening it for her. She gazed at him in open consternation, catching a look full of mocking knowledge. The violence of her raging emotions trembled through her, and she swept through the open door like a queen. As she walked with quick, angry strides to her car, she could only seethe at the cool amusement she had glimpsed on that hated face.

Savagely she swung her car door open, and seconds later she started the station wagon, waiting breathlessly for it to roar into action. She pulled out of the lot, refusing to look at the glittering dark eyes that she knew were following her. *Get out of my life,* she ordered silently. *Get out and stay out.*

Jeremy Boulanger stood watching Lindsey Wiltse drive away, asking himself what in the hell he was doing, springing himself on her like that. But he hadn't expected her to appear so...breakable. And she looked like just a kid; it was hard to believe she was twenty-seven years old.

Impatiently, he glanced at the thin gold watch at his wrist. Midnight, Michigan time. It had taken him exactly six hours to drive to this northern Michigan town, and he resented every minute of it. He would not give Mrs. Lindsey Wiltse an opportunity to use any more of his time than absolutely necessary. He would get this unfortunate business over with as soon as possible, and with as little cost as possible to himself.

Yes, he would do the job, and quickly. In the meantime he would try not to acknowledge the awful desolation he felt every time he thought of the other news: that his father would be dead soon, and he had never known him.

Later that night, Lindsey Wiltse lay troubled in her bed. She had reacted like a rebellious teenager, she scolded herself. She had let him see her surprise, her shock, her anger.

So what? she demanded silently. He can't hurt me, anymore than his father can. And if he was playing delivery boy with some further bribe from John Boulanger, she could tell him where to go fast enough.

She had thought, truly thought, that she had gotten over the old hatred and bitterness that had twisted her life so long ago. But when she had heard from Boulanger two months ago, she found that the old dormant feelings were awakened with a fierceness that she could not seem to suppress. And now, her modest flannel nightgown pulled over her slender frame, her body in enforced relaxation against her sheets, she could not sleep. Instead, she felt swamped by the old feelings of violent loathing she had buried for so many years. It did not help that her stomach felt empty, and she remembered with a faint shrug that she had not had dinner. She was simply too tired to crawl out of her warm blankets to fix something to eat. Her bedside clock's illuminated numbers clearly read one-thirty. Restlessly she turned, her fists in tight balls at her side. Sleep was coming hard tonight.

Two hours later Lindsey's rumpled bed was a mute witness to her tossing and turning. In utter frustration she banged her fist into her pillow. What was wrong with her? She needed this rest so desperately, tomorrow she would feel only too strongly her lack of it. No matter what had happened tonight, nothing so serious had occurred that she should be deprived of her precious rest.

Finally, in desperation, Lindsey allowed herself to remember.

She had just turned ten when she discovered her mother was not going to live at home anymore. Her mother had not been home in more than a week, and she finally had sought some answers from her father. She remembered the scene vividly. Her waist-length hair had been carefully braided, and she had been wearing a lacy pink blouse over a pair of darker pink corduroy pants. She had found her father in his study.

"Daddy, Daddy, where's Mom?" she had asked, her thin girlish voice confused and afraid.

"Darling..." Her solid redheaded father had swept her up in his strong, reassuring arms. "Mommy has gone away. She's not coming back."

His words shocked her. "Why, Daddy? Doesn't she love me anymore? Where did she go, Daddy?" His arms continued to hold her, but no answers were given to her questions. She became more demanding. "Daddy, I want my Mommy. Make her come back, Daddy. You can go and get her." Her little girl's voice had risen shrilly. "Make her come home. Make her come home, Daddy."

But her mother had never come home again, except for brief periods of time to see her daughter. Lindsey grew older, and as she grew she began to pattern herself after her father, dressing herself as much like a boy as possible. She had her hair cut in a blunt, masculine style.

Her mother had been appalled.

"Why won't you dress like a girl, Lindsey?" her mother had asked her.

"Why won't you leave me alone?" Lindsey had responded resentfully, her eyes hard and unforgiving as she had gazed upon the vision of feminine softness and beauty that was her mother.

"Lindsey, try to understand," her mother had pleaded. "John is so special. Please meet him. Try to like him, for my sake."

But Lindsey had not been able to bear it. She covered her ears with her hands and ran from the room.

Time had passed, and in the course of it, she had finally met John Boulanger. But even the neutral ground of an exclusive restaurant had not been able to blunt Lindsey's anger. Her rudeness had caused her mother to break into tears, and Boulanger had chastised her unmercifully.

Then, one crisp autumn day, when she was twelve, Lindsey had found her father unexpectedly waiting for her as she left the school building. One look at his ravaged face told her that something was wrong. "Lindsey," her father said in greeting, but his voice was like a stranger's.

"What is it, Daddy?" she asked, an odd breathlessness catching her throat.

"There has been an accident, honey." A flame of certain knowledge shot through her. Her eyes flew to her father's face, noting with dismay that he looked older and more haggard than she had ever seen him.

"Mother is dead, isn't she?" Surely that cold, heartless voice could not be her own.

"Yes." Nothing could disguise the raw agony in her father's face.

"What happened?" She leaned against their old pickup, half-turned from her father, her hard, adult expression contrasting oddly with her youthful features.

"She and Boulanger were returning from a weekend in Las Vegas." Her father's voice caught raggedly. "They had been drinking, and...they ran a red light." Her father clutched her convulsively. "She didn't suffer, Lindsey. She died instantly."

"And Boulanger?" she snapped.

"A few bruises." The older man took a jagged breath, his voice a whisper of bitter disbelief. "A few bruises."

"I hate him. I'll kill him," she cried forcefully.

"Lindsey..." His hands found her shoulders and he gave her a firm shake. "Listen to me. Your life is just beginning. Do not fill it with thoughts of hatred and revenge. Fill your life with what is good and beautiful. You have the world before you." Her father paused, as if uncertain how to continue. "As for me, my life is finished. I always thought maybe Ruth Ann would come back to me, but now there is no hope for that. Lindsey, forgive me, but I have nothing left to live for."

She gazed at him helplessly. "You have me, Dad. I'm worth ten of her. *You have me*." Her young hands grasped his surrounding arms with fierce strength.

The tears fell freely down the weakened features of the prematurely old man. "No." He sounded lost and defeated. "I love you, but the love of a father for his daughter is not enough, Lindsey." He seemed unaware that each word was a knife thrusting cruelly into her heart. "I can no longer continue. My life is nothing."

Slowly Lindsey became aware of the shrill sound of her bedside alarm. She turned groggily, half expecting to see her father's grief-stricken face at her side. As she gradually became aware of where she was, she groaned softly.

When had memory become so real? When had the past seemed so intertwined with the present? She drew in an uneven breath, only to find it ending in a choked sob. With uncharacteristic anger, she jerked the alarm from its plug and hurled it across her room, finding no satisfaction in the splintering sound it made against her bedroom wall.

Chapter Two

"Bother!" Lindsey murmured irritably as she tried for the fourth time to get Mr. Arnold's letter done on her word processor. She reached for the coffee that sat steaming on her desk, trying not to notice that her hand was trembling. She wrapped both hands around the warmth of her mug and sat for a moment, trying to relax the tension she had felt building in her throughout the day. When would he approach her again? What would he say? What would *she* say?

"Problem-solving, Lindsey?" Her distinguished-looking boss was standing quietly behind her.

"Oh...I'm sorry, Sam. I was just caught up in my thoughts for a moment," Lindsey explained hurriedly. She put her coffee back on her desk and dutifully turned again to Sam's letter.

"Is everything all right?" Sam Arnold's concern was evident in his slightly creased brow.

"Everything is just fine." Lindsey smiled apologetically. "I ran a little short of sleep last night, but I'm okay."

"That witch of a mother-in-law is not bothering you again, is she?" Her boss's questioning persisted.

"No, I haven't heard from Corrinne for some time now." Lindsey ran a careless hand through her hair. "It's just me, I'm afraid. I was just a little restless last night, I guess."

"Look, Lindsey..." Sam's voice was abnormally gruff. "I'll get one of the other secretaries to finish this afternoon. You go home and get some sleep."

Lindsey's eyes flew to Sam's face. "I'm really all right," she protested, her voice low. "I can finish out the day."

"Sure." Sam's voice was sharper than usual. "You have been working on that simple letter for forty-five minutes. At that rate you will do approximately fifteen minutes' worth of work during the next three hours."

Lindsey flushed at her boss's crisp tone. She had not been aware of him watching her. Now he softened noticeably as he viewed her obvious embarrassment. "Go home and get some rest." Sam's hand rested momentarily on her shoulder. "That is an order from the highest authority this company has."

Lindsey's eyes filled with tears. While inwardly she cursed her weakness, she could not deny the rush of gratitude she felt toward Sam Arnold. Impulsively she rose and put her arms around Sam's neck, and planted a quick kiss on his cheek.

"Thanks, Sam," she whispered huskily.

"And eat something," Sam muttered, his face reddening slightly. "You are as thin as a broom handle."

"Oh, Sam." Lindsey leaned her head against his broad chest, and felt the older man's arms surround her comfortingly. She discovered, to her shame, that she was crying in earnest now. What on earth was wrong with her, anyway? She had used to be so tough, ages ago. Grimly Lindsey remembered her self-description of the previous evening. Fragile. Breakable. She must be nearer to collapse than she had realized. With an almost superhuman effort she pulled out of Sam's arms, sniffing miserably, too embarrassed to meet his eyes. She must look a complete and total mess, she thought resignedly. Dully she took the handkerchief Sam was offering her and wiped her eyes.

"I don't know what you must think," Lindsey hesitated, seeking the right words to explain away her tears, but Sam cut her short with a rough gesture.

"You're pushing too hard, Lindsey." His tone held concern in its harshness. "And if you do not go home this minute and crawl into your bed for some obviously much-needed rest, I will fire you."

"Yes, sir, on the double, sir, anything you say, sir." Unfortunately Lindsey's efforts at flippancy sounded flat and weak. She gave her boss one watery, tremulous smile, grabbed her handbag and fled, unaware of Sam Arnold's troubled eyes following her out of the office doorway.

Later, Lindsey found herself unable to be completely obedient to Sam's dictates. Sleep in the afternoon seemed impossible. So, determinedly turning a blind eye to the dust that was thick on her shelves, Lindsey chose to relax in her bath for almost an hour. She treated her hair to a special rinse solution, and after toweling herself dry and applying bath powder liberally, she carefully applied mascara, blusher and a lipstick in a definitive shade of red.

Lindsey smiled at her reflection in the mirror. Then, because she was afraid to admit even to herself that this extra care about her appearance might have something to do with how bedraggled she had felt beneath the piercing blue eyes of the stranger in the doughnut shop last night, she found herself almost underdressing, pulling on a pair of slim-fitting casual navy slacks and a severely cut white blouse. Still, the leisure time and her consequently improved appearance made Lindsey move a little more gracefully than usual as she went through the motions of the evening: picking up her children at the sitter's, fixing dinner, waiting for her neighbor, Mrs. Owens, to appear so that she could leave again for her evening job.

As the minutes of preparation passed, Lindsey, drawing on the strength of mind that had helped her survive through the troubled times of her life, absolutely refused to think about the man who had so disturbed her the previous evening. Nor did she review the vivid recollections that had plagued her during the night. Instead, she kept her mind fixed firmly on the events at hand, smiling and laughing with Christopher and Catherine, and even spent extra time with them before bedtime. It was refreshing to feel so relaxed.

So it was, when Lindsey entered the doughnut shop that night, this time using the back entrance, her head was high and her eyes were clear. At the same time she felt an anger at her circumstances that lifted her chin defiantly. And the man sitting at the short counter watching for her arrival narrowed his eyes sharply as he observed her brightness. For he was there, as some sixth sense had been warning Lindsey all along that he would be, only this time he had not waited until closing, but instead he was sitting, waiting, and she knew he was there because of her.

For a moment cold rage racked her body. Turning from the counter, she managed a calm hello to Bobby Saunders, the young college kid who worked the shift before hers. She busied herself by removing her coat and boots, tying on her apron. Then she dared a glance at this man who had already become her adversary, hoping her face revealed nothing but a calm nonchalance.

Lindsey was kept busy for the first forty-five minutes of her shift, but all the time she was aware of him, knew that he was nursing his coffee along with a sweet roll that he had barely touched, and knew that his eyes rarely left her as she performed her work. He made her jittery, so that more than once she had to ask a customer to repeat his order, and she grew flustered, finding herself making incorrect change. He was getting to her, and she felt a slow burn of anger that he should be having this effect on her, that he should be here at all.

After that first glance she had tried not to look at him, but in spite of herself she was aware that he was wearing a dark blue sport shirt, open at the neck, revealing a V of thick growth on his chest. His strong, full lips were relaxed in a half-smile as he sat patiently on the little round counter stool.

In the end, it was the anger that saved her. She stopped trembling, and felt a welcome icy control envelope her. He had lost the advantage of surprise, and she was fully capable of handling whatever he chose to dish out. In fact, she felt more than ready to do a little dishing out, herself.

After a time the shop quieted so that she was left alone with the man whose intensely blue eyes had followed her so closely. She felt herself tense, as if in preparation for a battle, but she still refused to look at him, to acknowledge his presence in even the slightest way. She would let him make the first move. With her back to the room, she began to make a fresh pot of coffee.

"Lindsey." His voice, when it came, was as hard and arrogant as she had expected.

She finished making the coffee, then turned. "You know my name." It was a statement of fact, delivered in cool tones.

"Your name tag," he offered in explanation, playing her game of nonrecognition. His look became amusedly confident.

Filthy rich, she reminded herself bitterly, bristling instinctively. Expensive clothes, styled hair, arrogant voice, but it was the look that clinched it. Only the wealthy looked at people like that. John Boulanger had had money, but he had still acted like a tradesman. This one had been born with a silver spoon in his mouth. She tilted her chin coolly, saying nothing.

He startled her by smiling, and she noted somewhat uncomfortably the practiced charm which played across his features. "Your name is announced to anyone," he continued blandly, "by this." He reached across the counter to touch the tag on her blouse.

She refused to draw back, but something of what she was feeling must have crept into her expression, for a strangely satisfied gleam shone out of his blue-black eyes. She did not like that gleam, she did not like his smile, she did not like it when he touched her. She knew she did not imagine the supercilious lift to his eyebrow, as if he had examined her and found her wanting. Obviously, he did not much care for her either. That was just fine. Maybe he would turn around and leave so that she could forget she had ever seen him.

But she was to be disappointed, for he made no movement at all, either to walk out the door or simply to sit down again. Instead his gaze settled once again on her face. Lindsey met his stare with one of insolent disdain, and made a sudden decision to take the initiative after all.

She made her voice light and openly mocking. "You know," she said slowly, "you remind me of someone I once knew...a lifetime ago. He would have looked at women like that, too." She shrugged delicately, contemptuously. She gave him a smile, sweetly continuing. "But perhaps all you want is another sweet roll?" she asked, derisively hopeful.

She noted his stiffening back with some satisfaction, and anger flared in his eyes as he absorbed her insult. He shot her a look of cold dislike. "As I still have part of my last one—" he waved a negligent hand toward the space where he had been sitting, "—I don't think so." He continued bitingly, "But, lamentably, I do need something else."

She inclined her head haughtily, her mascara-coated lashes sweeping down to hide her sudden dismay. She thought he was going to explain the reason for his being there, and she found she did not really want to know. She dropped her pose and looked at him frankly.

"Look," she said abruptly. "I don't want to hear it, okay? Whatever the something else is, do me a favor and keep it a secret."

"But why should I do you any favors?" he asked, his smile taunting her. "And I think you already know that I have come for you." There was a glint of challenge in his electric blue eyes as he looked down at her. "I have come to take you to Chicago to see my father, John Boulanger."

It was as if time stood still. The deep blue eyes in that overwhelmingly masculine face clashed with Lindsey's gray ones, his look arrogant, inflexible, tenacious. Lindsey felt as if nothing in the world existed besides his eyes, and she would remember forever their shape, their brilliant color, but most of all the unmistakable sense of command that communicated itself to her through them. She stood, rigid, her entire universe shrunk to the space that held this man and herself in silent combat. It seemed as if he was establishing his innate superiority, his territory, and she was somehow included in what he claimed. Her face whitened, her lips curled, her nostrils widened slightly in a completely unconscious reaction to the threat she felt emanating from the set visage before her. Her eyes darkened and grew smoky, her dislike and resentment so tangible a force between them that the man would have to have been dead not to have felt the force of her feelings.

"I want nothing to do with your father." She heard her voice speaking as if from a great distance, and felt a moment of gratitude that it sounded calm and even, with no noticeable tremors. "Or with you. I find you detestable, but I expected nothing less . . . from a Boulanger."

His eyebrows shot up insolently, and his gaze raked her face. "So the little ragged kitten has claws." He made his voice soft, to match hers.

Furious, she refused to comment further. With an impatient shrug, she finally moved her eyes from his, and found herself wishing hotly that he would leave. She was not sure she was up to this explosive confrontation, even though she could feel the blessed adrenalin pumping through her veins. *Please, please let him go away.* The prayerful words formed in her brain, but none of the pleading weakness showed in her face as she held herself stiffly aloof, her sweetly molded chin tilted upwards.

The little bell tinkled above the front door of the doughnut shop, its ringing sounding absurdly merry in the strained atmosphere. She felt, rather than saw, the dark man move away so that she would be free to serve her customer. Her eyes flicked to the person who was entering the shop, and a welcome relief surged through her tightly strung body. Defiantly aware of the hard blue eyes that had never left her face, she shot a radiant smile at the newcomer.

"Robert Connor!" She breathed the name in grateful delight, and was rewarded with an answering grin from the blond giant. Robert was an old friend, a long-distance truck driver who never failed to look Lindsey up when he was in town for more than twenty-four hours. Never was Lindsey more thankful to see him, and she was not hesitant about revealing her pleasure. Bitterly aware that the Boulanger man had seated himself again at the counter, she impulsively held her hands out to Robert. "I'm so happy to see you!" she exclaimed, her voice low and huskily breathless.

Robert took her hands and squeezed them tightly in his own. Then he leaned leisurely over the white Formica counter that separated them. "Sunshine, such a smile I would drive a thousand miles for," he responded enthusiastically, before planting a great kiss firmly on Lindsey's lips.

"Robert!" she protested, laughingly pushing him away. "So how was California?"

Continuing to clasp her delicately boned hands in his own mammoth ones, Robert walked around to Lindsey's side of the counter. He took in her features hungrily. "California was fine," Robert answered her briefly. "But I don't need to ask how you are, Lindsey. I can see with my eyes the truth before me."

Bending his blond head toward her, Robert said tenderly, with a hint of ownership in his voice, "You are skin and bones, my dear. It hurts me to see you like this." Robert's gentle hands massaged her arms. "Your eyes were made for laughing, Lindsey. It is time you quit carrying a torch for Brad. You need help, and I want to be the one who provides it. Shoot, I make four times more money than I am spending."

"Robert..." She tried to halt his words, knowing that she could not accept what he was offering. Acutely aware of their unfriendly audience, Lindsey said quietly. "This is not the time or place for such a discussion, Robert."

"You are darned right about that," Robert said ruefully. "I didn't mean to get carried away, but then you don't know what your smile does to me, Lindsey. I reckon there isn't a woman alive who can match your face when it is lit up by your smile."

She was beginning to feel self-conscious, and more than a little guilty as she realized that she was using Robert to help her feel good in front of her piercing-eyed enemy. She looked at Robert gravely, making her voice calm and controlled. "You certainly are good for my ego, Robert."

"I should hope so," the blond man replied gallantly. "And I would like to be good for something else as well. Come out with me Saturday night, Lindsey. You deserve to have some fun."

Blazingly aware of the darker man sitting tightly coiled just a few feet away, Lindsey felt gratified that Robert, at least, could find her desirable in her present state. And it would be fun to go out. She had not done anything fun in such a long time. Lindsey refused to consider that her acceptance had anything to do with the fierce, penetrating eyes that had been staring at Robert and her with veiled hostility, with the way those eyes made her seem small and un-important.

Refusing to even glance in the direction of the other man, Lindsey looked directly at Robert and smiled again, that same luminous smile she had bestowed on him earlier. "I would like that very much, Robert," she accepted his invitation graciously.

Robert gazed at her face a moment longer, then squeezed her arms in silent promise. "Eight o'clock then," he suggested warmly. "That should give you enough time to have the wee ones in bed."

"Yes, all right," Lindsey replied.

Robert grinned engagingly, then turned to leave. He was whistling softly under his breath as he closed the door behind him, again setting off the cheery bell chimes. As the last bell sounded, Lindsey became almost suffocatingly aware of the tensely furious presence of the other man. She immediately missed Robert's comfortable, predictable presence as she again found herself alone with the man who had been lingering disturbingly under her many layers of conscious thought over the past twenty-four hours. She felt the physical pull of his steady regard, and angrily she turned to face him.

But Lindsey was not prepared for the fierce derision that she discovered in his night-blue eyes, and she was momentarily stunned into silence. Then strengthened with the knowledge of Robert's admiration and desire, she turned from the Boulanger man, tossing her head carelessly.

Surely she was not afraid of the man. Her face grew stony at the thought. And where were all her customers tonight? The presence of another human being would be a welcome buffer in this silent struggle of wills, but no one appeared to aid her.

Lindsey, with her back still turned to the counter, heard the man rise quietly, and she thought that he must, at last, be ready to leave. Straightening her shoulders, she waited for the sound of the door chimes to let her know that he had gone. The sound of quiet footsteps stopping, instead, close behind her filled her with fury. Why wouldn't he leave? Why was he pestering her in this manner? She turned, her gray eyes stormy with her agitation.

He was standing just inches from her, had joined her behind the counter where Robert Connor had stood just a short time ago. Only the slight darkening of her eyes betrayed her fear, but she felt ravaged by the tall man's intimidating proximity. Deliberately, she thrust her head back slightly, standing rigid and defiant as Jeremy's eyes touched her insolently.

"Mrs. Lindsey Wiltse." Jeremy's voice was soft and expressionless.

She gave a little gasp, and took a small step backward. Hearing her name on his lips was repugnant to her, and loathing flared in her eyes.

If he noticed her reaction he gave no sign. "Perhaps we ought to begin again," he continued. "My name is Jeremy Boulanger, and I have come here, as I said, for the express purpose of meeting you." He put out his hand, as if to shake hers.

"Well, you have met me," she whispered fiercely. "Now, get out of here."

His hand remained frozen in mid-air. He studied her assessingly. "You really are a surprise, Lindsey Wiltse. Not at all what I expected." With that, he reached out to touch her hair.

She felt burned. "Get your hand off of me," she ordered.

She saw again the light of battle in his eyes, and knew instinctively that she had said the wrong thing. "I haven't come all this way to trade insults," he said, "but since you find me so... detestable, I may as well return the favor."

The offending hand that was still on her hair stroked her head lightly. She jerked away.

"Don't you like being touched, Mrs. Wiltse?" he jeered. "Or is it only that my name is Boulanger?"

She remained stubbornly silent.

"So you have a friend who wants to help, Lindsey Wiltse," he continued, unheeding of her silence. "My father wants to help you, too, and you can bet he will have a lot fewer demands than your blond boyfriend."

"I don't want your father's money," she said slowly and distinctly. "And I don't want to talk with you."

There was an indication of thinning patience in the hardening of Jeremy's face, but his voice remained casually sardonic. "My father told me of your attitude. I confess I thought he might have exaggerated, but I see now he spoke the truth. You've got more pride than sense, Mrs. Wiltse," he continued insultingly, "but pride won't pay the rent. Nor will it put food on your table."

Her blazing anger made her sound more controlled than she was. "I pay my own rent and buy my own groceries, Mr. Boulanger."

"Pride won't pay for other things, either, Mrs. Wiltse." He thrust a computerized sheet on the counter beside them. It was headed "Wiltse, Lindsey," and under her name was a dismayingly accurate list of her assets and liabilities.

She tried not to look at that damning sheet of paper. Yet humiliation drained her, as in spite of herself, she stared at the all too clear facts of her disastrous monetary state. She tried to block out the sound of Jeremy's detached, impassive voice.

"You're in deep waters financially, Mrs. Wiltse. You're going to drown soon unless you get an inflow of cash. How proud will you be when your truck-driving friend starts forking over some of his hard-earned greenbacks to bail you out? What will you sell him in return?" Her eyes flashed angrily at his harsh words, but he continued mercilessly. "How about your children, Lindsey? Is your hatred of John Boulanger so strong that you will let them go without?" She was breathing deeply, fighting for control, when he dropped his final, most telling question.

"Will your hatred furnish the necessary funds for your son's operation, Mrs. Wiltse?"

She despised him. She despised that self-confident voice that pounded at her like a drumbeat from hell. She despised the fact that while she was struggling hard not to burst into tears, he was calm and untouched. She despised the masculine arrogance that came perilously close to provoking her blind agreement to everything he said.

But no amount of cold reason had been able to convince her to take money from John Boulanger, and she would not change her mind now.

She stiffened her spine and instilled a note of cynical indifference into her voice. "And no doubt you, being John Boulanger's son, think that money can buy you anything."

She paused, and met his hooded eyes straight on. "But not me. I'll not be bought. Not now. Not ever."

The chimes tinkled above the door, and a customer entered at last.

"Everybody has a price," Jeremy said. "I'll find yours. Until then, at least we know where we stand, don't we? I'll be seeing you, Lindsey Wiltse. Think of me, won't you?"

Her eyes spoke her wrath, but she remained obstinately silent. With an enigmatic half-smile that revealed nothing of what he was feeling, Jeremy finally turned to go. It was not until Lindsey heard the powerful revving of his car that she was able to relax, and she found with a start that she was trembling.

Hating all Boulangers more than ever, she turned to serve the customer who stood waiting for her attention.

Chapter Three

"I'll set the table, Mommy," seven-year-old Catherine offered generously. "I'm all dressed and ready." Lindsey looked up from where she was tying Christopher's special oxfords. "That would be great, honey," she said gratefully, surveying her daughter with pleasure.

Catherine was lovely—with huge black eyes fringed with luxuriant eyelashes and hair longer and thicker than any seven-year-old deserved to have. With her smooth child's complexion, Catherine promised to be a real beauty as she grew older. But her true beauty was her spirit, which radiated happiness and compassion unusual in one so young.

Lindsey was determined to shield Catherine and her younger brother Christopher from anything in life that would take from them the innocence and happiness that they seemed to accept as their birthright. *Let them be happy. That is my legacy to them. The security of happiness, of knowing that they are loved and important.*

Lindsey quickly finished with Christopher, fastening his special braces in place over his shoes, then pulling on his loose-fitting pants. Swinging Christopher into her arms, she hurried to the kitchen, where she sat him in front of a bowl of cold cereal. "I'll be back in a minute, sweethearts," Lindsey said. "Go ahead and begin eating."

With a quick turn, Lindsey practically ran down the hall, glancing nervously at her watch as she did so. There was just enough time to apply a little bit of makeup and pull on her dress. She was applying lipstick when she heard a loud crash in the kitchen, followed by an ear-splitting scream. Catherine's voice was unnaturally loud as she called, "Mommy!"

"Christopher!" Lindsey exclaimed, covering the short distance from bedroom to kitchen in record time. She found her son sprawled on the faded linoleum, a half gallon container of milk pouring its remains in a puddle that had quickly seeped underneath him. His chair was overturned, and the plastic bowl that had held Christopher's breakfast cereal was on the floor, upside down, blending its contents with the pale yellow of his hair. Catherine had already pulled a towel out of the cupboard and was trying to stop the flow of milk across the kitchen floor.

"Oh, Christopher," Lindsey murmured, her heart fragmenting at the sight of Christopher's tear-stained face, with its mixture of little boy hurt and adult rage as he tried to pull himself to his feet. Unheeding of the milk and cereal remains that squished beneath her shoes, Lindsey bent to pick up her son.

"I just wanted some more milk, Mommy," he explained through the hiccups that always accompanied his tears, "but my legs got all tangled up."

Take three deep breaths, Lindsey ordered herself. Smile. Don't let them see how upset you are.

She reached out a hand and touched Catherine's shoulder. "Don't try to clean up this mess, honey. I think it's a little beyond you. Go ahead and finish getting ready. I'll get Christopher changed." Lindsey was pleased with the tone of calm cheerfulness she had achieved.

She carried Christopher to the bathroom. Working as quickly as she could, she stripped Christopher's milk-sodden clothes off and threw them into the bathtub. She washed his face and wiped down his hair, then forced herself to allow him to walk on his own steam into the bedroom where they found him new clothes. He had quit crying.

"I wish my legs worked like Mike's," he now said wistfully, referring to the four-year-old who lived next door.

Lindsey caught her lip with her teeth. Born with clubfeet, Christopher had spent all of his life in braces. "Your legs will work better, Chris," she reassured firmly. "They are already miracle legs, you know."

"I don't want miracle legs," Christopher replied, sniffing. "I want legs like Mike's."

Glancing again at her watch, Lindsey took Christopher by the shoulders and looked into his eyes. "They will work better," she repeated with emphasis, "but right now we are running late. Let's go back to the kitchen and get you some more cereal, shall we?"

A short while later, Lindsey watched out the window as Catherine caught the bus at the corner. It was only moments before she had Christopher's winter coat on him and was buckling him in her station wagon. The sitter's house was a scant two miles away, and after dropping Christopher there, she turned the Ford in the direction of her office.

Lindsey forced herself to take a deep breath. Her morning schedule, forced into regularity by the arrival of Catherine's school bus, usually ensured that Lindsey arrived at work ten minutes early, but the upset with Christopher had put her just that much behind. Lindsey grimaced at herself in the car's mirror as she realized that she had also—again—neglected to eat. It was not a very good beginning to the day, but she had handled worse.

Indeed, the late dash to work and the nonexistent breakfast were mere trifles, Lindsey thought bitterly, compared to the events of the previous evening. Her knuckles whitened as they gripped the steering wheel. Her entire body felt hot at the memory of her confrontation with Jeremy Boulanger.

The worst part of it all was the hate. She had been so sure she was incapable of feeling that terrible hatred anymore, and here it was, back in full force. Long ago, she had allowed that hatred to practically destroy her. Only her husband, Bradley, had been able to see the person she was behind the wall of rebellion she had built around herself, and if it weren't for him...Lindsey chewed her lip worriedly. Bradley had saved her life, and then he had given her a love that she had neither deserved nor, at first, had wanted. Now it seemed that his efforts, his genuine goodness, had been for nothing; the malice she felt for Jeremy Boulanger was just as ugly an emotion as any she had directed toward her mother and John. It even made her feel like hating herself.

Several hours later, Lindsey was determinedly finishing typing a multi-paged report that was to be delivered to one of Arnold's biggest and most important clients. She ignored her stomach, which had been trying to remind her of its empty state for some time now. When her desk phone rang, Lindsey picked it up absently, still concentrating on her work. "Lindsey Wiltse here." She spoke briskly into the receiver.

"Good morning, Mrs. Wiltse," drawled a calm, masculine voice. "I wondered if—"

Lindsey slammed down the phone as if it were a flaming brand. How dare he? What right had this arrogant man, a perfect stranger, to interrupt her concentration like this? She stared, horrified, at the black desk telephone, as if expecting Jeremy Boulanger to materialize in its place. But she had not actually talked with him. That, at least, was some satisfaction. And that was exactly what she would continue to do, she thought with sudden clarity. She would simply refuse to have anything to do with him.

It was a little after three o'clock in the afternoon when Lindsey heard the stir of excited conversation from the direction of the secretarial pool. She was in the process of taking dictation from Sam Arnold, and looked up to find his questioning eyes on her.

"Something going on that I don't know about?" Sam asked her, referring to the unusual commotion that seemed to be approaching his outer office.

She gave him an expressive shrug. "If there is, it's a surprise to me, too," she replied, then turned slightly as Sam's office door opened.

"Oh, Mr. Arnold..." Pamela Goodman, the company receptionist, was standing in the doorway. "I didn't mean to disturb you, but Lindsey has got a delivery. She is supposed to sign for it herself." Pamela paused expectantly.

"By all means, Lindsey, see what it is," Sam Arnold said kindly.

Puzzled, Lindsey left his office to go to her desk. Several of the office staff were standing around her work area. Now the faces of her co-workers were turned in her direction, delighted curiosity plainly written on their faces. For planted atop her desk were the most gorgeous roses Lindsey had ever seen—a full three dozen of them. A shiver of premonition swept through her, and she felt suddenly cold. The delivery boy handed Lindsey an envelope.

"There is a message, Mrs. Wiltse. I'm to wait for an answer," he said, grinning.

Maybe they are from Robert Connor, Lindsey thought hopefully. This was just the crazy, generous kind of thing he would do. But she knew even as she turned the little white envelope in her hands that the roses were not from Robert. She opened the card slowly, not hearing the teasing comments from the people around her. The bold, slashing handwriting seemed to jump out at her. *I'm sorry. Can I make amends by taking you to dinner tonight?* The signature was a stark, *Jeremy*.

Lindsey felt her face go bright red, and knew her audience had mistaken the blush for one of pleasure when she heard their amused responses.

"Who's it from, Lindsey?"

"You been keeping something secret?"

"Come on, Lindsey, aren't you going to answer your secret admirer?"

Finally, something of the anger she was feeling must have shown on her face because the light laughter and friendly teasing that had surrounded her gradually faded into an embarrassed silence. The delivery boy shifted uncomfortably.

With calm, disciplined movements, Lindsey turned the vase of roses upside down in her garbage receptacle. Then she took the note and tore it into neat quarters. She handed the tidy scraps of paper to the uniformed delivery boy.

"Give that to Mr. Boulanger," she said evenly. She eyed the upturned flowers with scowling displeasure. "And be sure to tell him what I did to his roses."

"Yes, ma'am," the messenger said meekly.

Ignoring the startled, curious faces encircling her, Lindsey turned to Sam Arnold, who was watching her quizzically. "I'm ready to continue with that dictation, Mr. Arnold," she said formally.

"Sure thing, Lindsey," he murmured, and together they returned to his office. Lindsey's rigidly controlled features seemed to prevent Sam from asking any questions, and he did not mention the roses to her for the rest of the day, although once or twice she saw him eyeing her questioningly.

Pamela Goodman shared none of Sam's polite reticence, however. Lindsey met Pamela in the coatroom at the end of the day. In fact, she had the distinct impression Pamela had been waiting for her, and she smiled wryly when Pamela asked, "All right, Miss Dark Horse, we are all dying to know what it's all about. Who is he?"

Lindsey knew it was probably fruitless to hope that she could ignore Pamela's questions indefinitely. Nevertheless, she tried to put Pamela off.

"Really, Pamela, I would rather not talk about it," she said firmly, and headed out to the parking lot.

Pamela kept pace with her. "Is he tall, dark and handsome?" she teased Lindsey. "Ooooo, Lindsey," Pamela murmured next, "is that him? Is that the man who sent you roses? Are you fighting with *him*?"

And he was there, leaning against a silver Porsche that was parked strategically next to her own ancient vehicle. Lindsey felt herself go pale with shock, then hot with explosive anger. He looked very casual, very masculine, very rich and very, very visible. She had meant to have her emotions under control when she saw him again. She had determined not to give way to her baser, uglier feelings about him; after all, it would only injure herself to hate again like in the old days. No, she had planned to rise above him, like some grand lady would rise above an ant, or maybe a lizard. But he was there, and she had not expected him. He had caught her unawares, and therefore she was disgustingly unprepared. She felt like shrieking at him.

She saw Jeremy straighten when he recognized her. His eyes were blue pinpoints of electricity that held Lindsey's own gaze captive.

This was too much. Obviously the man did not know how to accept a refusal. He was becoming a regular nuisance, and Lindsey comforted herself by remembering that she *had* dealt with nuisances before. She stiffened, straightening her back to give the illusion of added height. Her chin came up, and while she managed to keep her face expressionless, she could not help the darkening of her gray eyes as they reflected her anger. Purposefully, she strode toward her car.

Jeremy watched her approach, amusement etched across his features. He stood, his hands in the pockets of his gray wool slacks, his black trench coat left open to fly in the March winds, a tuneless whistle blowing between his teeth.

Lindsey was aware of everything about him, and she knew his appreciative glance was taking in her anger and defiance, even though she was trying so hard to keep her emotions hidden. The problem was her feelings were not under control at all, and the fire of battle was raging wildly in her heart by the time she reached her car. He was so close, she could smell his fragrance, could hear his breathing. Still, she gave no sign of recognition; her plan was to cut him dead.

Unfortunately, it was not his plan. "Hello," Jeremy said calmly, for all the world as if they met like this every day.

"Get out of my way," Lindsey said tersely, then cursed herself for revealing her tension. She jerked at her door handle. His hand shot out to encircle her wrist in a vicelike grip.

"I want to talk with you." Jeremy's voice was still light and slightly amused. The contrast could not have been greater between that light, friendly voice and the iron grip that she was sure was bruising the skin at her wrist.

The fire burning beneath the surface flared. Angrily Lindsey jerked her wrist in a circular motion, easily tearing it out of his grasp. Amazement momentarily flickered in his eyes, and while Jeremy did not try to regain his hold on her, he did move so that his considerable frame was leaning against her car door. The thought of his immaculate, costly clothes leaning against her dusty wagon made her smile briefly, and his thick dark brows rose in questioning response.

Instantly she turned from him to go around the hood of her car to get in on the passenger side. She would not spar with him. Once she lost control there was no telling what she would do. She would simply ignore him and get on her way. But Lindsey had not considered her actions clearly, for by the time she had swung herself into the seat, Jeremy had climbed into the driver's side. He met her furious gray eyes steadily, a glint of impatience in his own blue-black depths.

"Give me your keys, Lindsey," he ordered softly.

"Go to the devil," she answered chillingly.

He ignored both her answer and her mood. "I am taking you to dinner so we can talk. Since I doubt that I can get you into my car, we'll go in yours."

For a long moment Lindsey neither moved nor spoke. The silence stretched out uncomfortably, filling the spaces of the car, making breathing difficult and thinking impossible. She had to get control. That was the problem. This man assumed control with the ease of long practice, and it put her at an unfair disadvantage, caused her to feel weak and malleable.

Finally she turned her head from where she had been staring unseeing out the windshield to glance quickly around the parking lot. She saw that Pamela was already driving off, and that the lot was empty. It was her own fault, really. She had stayed late to avoid the questioning of her co-workers, and only Sam was left in the office. He would probably work for at least another hour. She could expect no help in human form.

At last she turned to look at Jeremy Boulanger, who had been sitting and watching her, cool amusement in his dark eyes. "My father was right," he said, "You really do hate all things Boulanger. You even hate me, though I had absolutely nothing to do with your mother and my father." He allowed a dismissive glance to flick over her. "That was a long time ago, little girl. One would have thought you'd have grown up by now."

That hurt, especially because he was partly right. It reminded her of something Bradley had once said: "You hated as a child, Lindsey. You're a woman now, and it's time to put away childish things. You can grow out of your hate."

She sat against the worn fabric of the car seat, clenching and unclenching her hands. She was sorry. Sorry, sorry, sorry. She guessed she never had grown up, because the hate was still there, like a stone around her heart.

Why had John Boulanger chosen this most challenging time of her life to track her down? Why had he sent his son to talk with her? The whys battered at her conscious thought, and with an effort she shoved them away. She folded her hands primly in her lap and decided to make an attempt at being the one in charge.

"Mr. Boulanger," she began in her most self-assured voice.

"Jeremy," he corrected with an underscore of mockery.

"Mr. Boulanger," she repeated stormily. "I resent your presence in my car almost as much as I resent your presence in my life. I want you out of both right now." She looked at him hard, then glanced away at the lazy amusement that lit his eyes. "You're nothing but a messenger boy, anyway. I won't deal with you or your father," she snapped conclusively.

Jeremy sat patiently, the fingers of his left hand rhythmically drumming against her steering wheel. He said nothing.

She felt her control slip.

"Please go," she tried, searching for the right tone of polite command. "I really do need to pick up my children." She met his long challenging look evenly, and was rewarded by a tightening of his mouth. She understood, at last and with relief, that he was bothered by the situation also, that he was not as sure of himself as he seemed. Good! She tried not to fidget or show restlessness in any way. Her will was as strong as his, she thought furiously. He could make the first move.

"I ought to leave, Lindsey Wiltse," he almost snarled. "You want nothing to do with me, and I—" he looked at her contemptuously, "—surely want nothing to do with you.

But my father sent me to help you, which I fully intend doing. However, I refuse to discuss the matter within the confines of this . . ." He looked disdainfully at her cluttered car, taking in the worn and frayed upholstery and the dusty dashboard, "rattletrap."

"Not all of us had silver spoons, Mr. Boulanger," she retaliated sweetly. "Besides, I like my car," she lied. "However, I agree with you. This is not the place for a discussion between us. Neither is anyplace else. So, go. Please, go. Tell your father you gave your best shot, and all that. But the lady simply wasn't willing. I'm sure you have better things to do, back in Detroit, or wherever."

"Chicago," he bit out.

"Yes, well, wherever." Her light tone hid the inner tension she was feeling. "If you would just open that door and scoot over to your little silver toy, you could get going, and so could I."

For an eternity Jeremy just sat looking at her. Looking down his supercilious nose, she would think later. She refused to drop her own eyes. She was so intent on the battle of wills between them that when his hand came out to touch her cheek, she jumped away, like a startled fawn.

He smiled grimly. "That's better," he murmured, as his fingers snaked out to grasp her chin. Her eyes again flew to his face, even as she raised her hand to bat his fingers away. He only tightened his hold, as his other hand came out to capture her two smaller ones and hold them still against his leg. Her chest constricted so that it was hard to get enough air. He studied her in evident satisfaction.

"Did you take classes in the art of intimidation?" she forced herself to ask lightly. "Or maybe you wrote the course?" She was ready for anything, she reassured herself, but when he threw back his head and gave a great shout of laughter, she was stunned into further silence. It quite transformed his face, that laugh, softening the harsh planes and hinting at a vulnerability underneath his cold exterior.

Taking a deep breath, she took advantage of his momentary softening. "Mr. Boulanger, why won't you just go away?"

"Because I'm taking you to dinner," he shot back.

"I can't go to dinner with you."

"Why not?"

"Christopher and Catherine, of course," she said, thinking to confound him.

"Ah. Your children. Let's see: Christopher is three, Catherine seven, right?"

Her anger flared anew. How was it he knew so much about her? Not only the ages of her children, but where she worked. Her financial obligations. What else was he aware of? She was trying so hard not to lose her temper that she failed to notice his own slight discomposure for several seconds. When she did notice, it was with the realization that Jeremy might have known about her children, but had not taken them into consideration in terms of dinner. She felt vaguely triumphant.

"Christopher and Catherine expect me to pick them up."

Silence again. She sat quietly, allowing her hands to stay imprisoned in his grip, fighting impulses to behave in ways she thought she had forgotten. Lindsey dared a glance at Jeremy's face, and saw a mask of such dark hostility there that for a moment she was startled. It was not as if she had asked him to come for her, after all!

For a moment Lindsey stared moodily out the windshield at the gray and white landscape. Somewhere the scene registered in her brain: the trees stripped bare of life, waiting for spring, the layer of snow that covered everything. She shivered.

His hand dropped from her chin, but he still kept her own fingers imprisoned against the length of his thigh. "Lord, this is out of hand," he murmured.

She looked at him unforgivingly. "I'd like my hands back," she said stiffly. He loosed them immediately.

"Look, Lindsey Wiltse. I admit I may have been somewhat . . . unorthodox. To tell you the truth, I had no desire
to come here on my father's behalf, and you've hardly been
pleasant yourself. But I won't leave without at least talking
with you." His voice turned persuasive, coaxing. "What will
it take to get you to talk with me, Lindsey? Isn't there some
hole in your admittedly busy schedule that you could find
in order to go to dinner with me?"

Why was he so determined to wine and dine her? she
thought distractedly. Maybe he thought she would soften up
over candlelight. Get rid of him, her warning voice urged.
She had to remember who he was and how he had humiliated her last night. She didn't dare to think for a moment he
had her best interest at heart. And never, never for a minute would she allow herself to think about how he looked
when he laughed, so vulnerable.

Vulnerable? Lindsey brought herself up short. If anyone
was vulnerable, it was she, not this too self-confident man
who had stalked her mercilessly from the first moment he
had set eyes upon her. Probably he had women falling all
over him everywhere he went—that was why he couldn't
hear her refusals. He had behaved abominably, and now he
thought that with a miserable excuse of an apology and a
few soft words he could storm her defenses.

"Mr. Boulanger," Lindsey said at last, her voice low and
scornful. "I have two children you have already made me
late picking up. I have precious little time to spend with
them, and nothing, absolutely nothing, would induce me to
spend time with you that I could be spending with them. As
I already suspect you know—" her voice was heavy with
accusation, "—I go to the Donut Shop at eight o'clock. I
have no time for going out whatsoever. I am a working single parent, not that you would even begin to understand the
responsibility such a role entails. But for the last time, I
don't care how far you have come or how much it has cost
you, I have nothing to say to you."

Jeremy's eyes had narrowed during her rebellious speech, so that no hint of kindness could be seen in them now. Indeed, his whole body seemed tightly coiled, as if only by the greatest self-control was he refraining from shaking her. That suited her mood fine. She did not want him to be considerate, or repentant, or nice. He was her enemy, and the faster she could convince him to leave her alone, the better off she would be.

"We could bring your children with us, Lindsey," Jeremy said, deliberately ignoring her other comments. "They might enjoy a dinner out also."

"No," she said, her voice tight with anger.

"You could invite me to your home, then," he continued, relentlessly reasonable.

Later her face would burn from the memory, but now she was tired and fed up with arguing with Jeremy Boulanger. Her body ached with exhaustion, and her spirit was wounded from the effort of fighting this man. That he should suggest that she invite him into her home was beyond mere insult. The sheer insolence of the man infuriated her, and she could think of nothing she could do that would force him to recognize her right to refuse to have anything more to do with him.

"It will be a cold day in hell when you step foot in my home, messenger boy," she spat in a low, boiling voice.

A brutal hand again grasped her chin, giving her head a merciless shake as Jeremy uttered sarcastically, "It's cold right now, and this is sure not heaven." A new, dangerous light appeared in his eyes. "Maybe it's time I melted a little ice."

No warning was given as his mouth swooped down against hers. Shock held her temporarily immobile as his lips parted hers with shameful ease. She felt his unconditional invasion, his absolute determination.

But, most horrifying of all, she felt her own unwilling response. She could not understand herself. Yet it was magnificent, this sensation of wonder and hunger.

His kiss changed. Domination became seduction, and through a mist of singing emotions, she heard the message there: *I will comfort your body and your heart. Let me. Let me.*

Was this what her own mother had yielded to years ago? At the thought, Lindsey began to struggle. But she was too weak, too open. Jeremy moved his arms to surround her, easily stilling the fluttering movements she made.

Panic seized her. She stiffened and raised her hands to push against his chest. She felt him pause against her lips. "What?" he asked, his voice incredibly tender.

Just like his father must have sounded. She began to understand how her mother might have succumbed.

But not her. She knew too much. Experience had no words with which to lie.

In a sudden riot of distressed movement, Lindsey tore herself out of Jeremy's grasp. She moved against the door, as far away from him as space would permit.

"No," she said.

"To what question?" his veiled but watchful look was studying her reaction.

Tears of bitter resentment stinging her eyes, she refused to meet his gaze. "All of them," she answered. "Go away."

"Talk to me, Lindsey Wiltse. Have dinner with me."

She was trembling. "I won't. You have damaged me, you and your father. I want to get on with my life." It was a plea more than a demand.

Lindsey saw a nerve twitch along Jeremy's jawline and sensed that he was holding some powerful emotion in check. Her gaze fixed on the second button of his shirt. "Will you go now?" It was appalling how unsure she sounded.

"Yes," he answered her shortly. "But don't think I'm leaving because I'm done, Lindsey Wiltse. We have unfinished business, you and I." Jeremy got out of her station wagon, but before he shut the door, he put his head down and gave a parting shot. "And, if you have time to go out with your yellow-haired truck driver, you have time to go out with me. You will go out with me, Lindsey Wiltse."

I wish he would quit saying my name like that, Lindsey thought angrily. But you are wrong. I'll never go out with you, Jeremy Boulanger, no matter what.

Saturday night found Lindsey looking forward almost feverishly to her date with Robert Connor. She had dressed with extra care. This was the first time she had gone out in months, and she wanted to look her best. She wore a soft dress of midnight blue, the simple style minimizing her thinness. An exquisite pearl necklace with accompanying earrings, a gift from Brad on their third anniversary, emphasized her face. She had applied makeup carefully, skillfully drawing attention to her deep-set eyes. Her shoulder-length hair swung loose and free about her face. And as a finishing touch she had applied a light dab of perfume behind her ears and at her elbows. The overall effect was one of youth and innocence, causing her to blink at her reflection. She almost wished Jeremy Boulanger could see her now.

Her hand stilled against her side. Flushing, Lindsey remembered the lengthy shower she had taken when she arrived home last night. It had been a vain effort to wash away the feel of Jeremy Boulanger's hands on her body. Now it seemed as if it was just as hopeless to try to cleanse her mind of his assault on her spirit.

In the three plus years since Bradley had died, Lindsey had felt little interest in other men, and thus her dates had been few. In fact, Bradley was the only man she had ever really dated.

A picture of herself when she had first met Bradley flashed before her. She had been in a kind of halfway house, along with several other wards of the state, although she had been the only orphan there. Bradley had been the social worker assigned to her case.

Bradley had been young and idealistic, and had been challenged by her absolute refusal to trust anyone. He had spent an extraordinary amount of time with her, and as her fear had lessened, she had showed him all her hurt and rage.

It had not been an easy time. She had cursed him for months, but he had never given up believing in her, and finally Lindsey had found herself deeply in love with this man who had seen something in her no one, least of all herself, had recognized. When he had offered marriage, she had been ecstatic, and it was not until later that she realized that Bradley had his own, unconquerable problems, stemming from a background that had been completely different than hers.

Months after their quiet wedding she had discovered that his family was part of the social register of Philadelphia. Disapproving of their son's choice of a mate, his parents had completely disowned him.

"Don't worry about it," Bradley had reassured her. "They haven't been exactly pleased with me for years."

Explaining further, he had told Lindsey that his father had expected him to take over the family business, and had become livid when Brad had refused to do so. "My choice of working with troubled youth was an offense to my parents," he had said lightly, "but I liked it, so I did it."

Then Bradley, thirty-one years old, had died of a totally unexpected heart attack. Lindsey's stomach still tightened at the memory of Bradley's funeral, and of what had come after.

Her mother-in-law had put in an appearance, accompanied by Bradley's younger brother, James. The older Mrs. Wiltse had gotten straight to the point.

"Give me the children," she demanded of an obviously pregnant Lindsey.

"What?" Lindsey had asked.

"Can you support them? What can you give them? I'm sure it will be a relief for you not to have the responsibility for two children when you go selling your wares a second time."

Horrible woman. Inhuman witch.

But it had been hard, supporting the children. Months after the funeral she finally realized just how unprepared she had been to handle life alone. Bradley, dealing with his own hidden wounds, had loved her so protectively that she had never had the need to drive a car or balance a checkbook. She had never worked at a paying job. She had married Bradley right after she had graduated from high school, and he had wanted her to stay home and raise their family. But he had not expected to die so young. He had not even bothered to take out any life insurance. The first year after he had died had been a nightmare of grief and helplessness for Lindsey.

Yet even in her darkest moments, Lindsey could not bring herself to hate Bradley. He had been everything to her: her father, her brother, her lover, her friend. She owed him, and she owed his memory respect and loyalty.

But it wasn't disrespectful to learn life's lessons. Trust could be given only rarely, and dependency never at all. All the men in her life left her, one way or the other, just when she had learned to depend on them. Now she depended on herself.

She sat quietly on her bed, waiting for the doorbell to announce Robert Connor's arrival. She found she really did not want to go, after all.

Perhaps there was no other man for her besides Bradley, imperfect as he had been. If only Bradley were still alive, her life would not be the mess it was now. *You fool,* Lindsey silently berated herself. *Bradley is dead. All the if onlys in the world cannot change that. And part of the mess you're in is Bradley's fault. Don't romanticize him.*

Unbidden, a dark-haired, blue-eyed image floated in front of her. She knew as surely as the sun rose each morning that she had not seen the last of Jeremy Boulanger. Unwelcome, resented, his final words to her echoed in her mind. "You will go out with me, Lindsey Wiltse."

As the doorbell rang, she stood determinedly, uncomfortably aware that her thoughts would be far from Robert Connor tonight.

Chapter Four

The rest of the weekend passed with no further word from Jeremy. Monday morning went smoothly, and Lindsey was able to deliver Christopher to the sitter's five minutes early. She utilized the extra time by stopping by her landlord's. It was necessary to explain that her rent, while late, would be paid, and this errand was a task that Lindsey dreaded. Nevertheless, she required herself to make her explanations in person, feeling somehow that this was the more honorable course to take. Her face was flushed with anticipated embarrassment as she knocked on Mr. Cook's door.

"Hello," Lindsey said a little awkwardly, when the stern-faced man answered her summons a few seconds later.

"Good morning, Mrs. Wiltse," Mr. Cook answered her greeting with stiff formality. "Won't you come in?"

Her hands perspiring, Lindsey walked into the Cooks' immaculate living room.

"Mr. Cook," she began hesitantly. "I stopped by to let you know that, well... I won't have the April first rent money, on the first I mean. But," she rushed on when her landlord would have interrupted, "I will be able to bring it to you by the fifteenth, if that is all right?" She hated the uncertainty in her voice. Coming to see Mr. Cook like this had taken the hope right out of her morning, and she stood, miserably studying the pattern in her landlord's carpet, waiting for his response.

"There is no need for you to worry at all, Mrs. Wiltse." Mr. Cook's words caused her to relax a little, until she heard his explanation. "Your rent has already been taken care of."

"W-what?" Lindsey stammered, her eyes searching the short man's blunt features.

"Yes." Mr. Cook nodded affirmatively. "Not only this month but next month has been paid also." She wondered if she was imagining a sly curiosity behind his customarily bland appearance.

"Who paid it?" Lindsey asked, her face white and set.

Mr. Cook allowed himself a small, knowing smile. "Why, Mr. Boulanger did, Mrs. Wiltse. He said he would be taking care of all your needs from now on." He paused delicately. "Perhaps you two will be making an announcement in the near future?"

If she had felt anger before it was nothing compared to the violent rage that flashed like a lightning bolt through her. "Oh no, Mr. Cook, there will be no announcement."

Her landlord's eyes brightened inquisitively.

"Look, Mr. Cook," Lindsey said briskly, in control once again. "I do not want Mr. Boulanger paying my rent. He did not ask my permission to do so, and in fact, I have no idea how he even knew your name. But under any circumstances, I will not have him paying my rent. You will just have to give him the money back. I know I will be late in April, but you know I have always paid you, plus I take good care of the house..."

Mr. Cook was shaking his head. "Now, Mrs. Wiltse," he placated her. "Your young man said you might react this way. He said you were too independent by far. As for giving him his money back, well, that would be difficult, seeing as he paid in cash, and I have neither his address nor his phone number. Besides, Mr. Boulanger said that under no circumstances was I to take a penny of your money, either now or in the future.''

The balding man paused for breath, seeming to take a degree of satisfaction in Lindsey's stunned expression. ''Mr. Boulanger is quite a gentleman, Mrs. Wiltse, if I may say so. I was very impressed with him. You could do worse.''

Worse than what? Lindsey thought fiercely. Worse than being Jeremy Boulanger's mistress? That was obviously what Mr. Cook thought. She tried again.

''But, Mr. Cook, I can't possibly allow Mr. Boulanger to pay my rent like this. I hardly know the man.''

''That you will have to discuss with him, Mrs. Wiltse.'' Her landlord looked impossibly stubborn. ''After all, with him paying, I have my money. As you have said yourself, that is more than you can accomplish.''

Burning hot, Lindsey turned abruptly and stormed out of Mr. Cook's front door. So Jeremy knew who her landlord was. What else did he know about her? With sudden clarity, Lindsey realized that with all the information Jeremy had about her, he must surely know a simple thing like where she lived. She clenched her hands at the thought that Jeremy Boulanger could suddenly appear on her doorstep. Demanding payment, she thought. Bribing her to go to Chicago.

Well, she'd pay him back, every penny, she vowed. She was not a charity case, and she would not be bribed to accommodate him. Just because he had money did not mean he could walk roughshod all over her life. If it was war that man wanted, he would find in her one soldier who would not be beaten.

But it was difficult to fight a hidden enemy. Jeremy made no further effort to contact her, and by Wednesday Lindsey was chaffing at her inability to straighten out the matter of her rent payments. Every time she thought of Mr. Cook's words she felt hot with embarrassment. That the little man should think that she and Jeremy were lovers was intolerable.

Wednesday afternoon Lindsey took some time off in order to accompany Christopher to a checkup at the doctor's. Dr. Stanford, a bone and foot specialist, was a gruff man in his mid-forties. He appeared pleased with Christopher's progress.

"He's doing well," he told Lindsey. "We should be looking at scheduling his surgery in about three months. You should start making arrangements now to take Christopher to Ann Arbor."

She nodded vaguely.

On her way out of the doctor's office, Lindsey stopped by the receptionist's desk. What she could pay today would not even cover the cost of the office visit, let alone make a dent in her very sizable account here. She sighed as she pulled out her check register.

"I'm sorry this is so small," she apologized to the receptionist. "But it is all that I can do, today."

"That is fine, Mrs. Wiltse," the petite, dark-haired woman replied.

"Maybe you could tell me the size of my balance?" Lindsey felt duty-bound to ask.

The receptionist flipped her file open. "Why, Mrs. Wiltse, your balance has been paid in full." She smiled. "You must have forgotten."

Forgotten?

When Lindsey returned to her office she placed a quick call to the hospital, where she had a very large, very late bill. With a sinking heart, she heard the now-familiar story. Her account, never entirely paid since Bradley's death, had been completely cleared.

Now that she wanted to talk to Jeremy, Lindsey could not reach him. Her attempts to locate him at any of the likely hotels or motels proved fruitless. No one by the name of Boulanger had registered at any of them. She tried Chicago information. The number was unlisted, the operator told her. She fumed helplessly, and she thought that this was probably just the effect Jeremy Boulanger wanted to have.

She had rehearsed over and over the speech she would give to Jeremy when she saw him. She would be Miss Cool next time. And she would win. She would make him understand that he must leave her alone.

Friday morning Lindsey dressed and fed Catherine and Christopher with quick, nervous movements. She had still not heard from Jeremy, and her inability to confront him was making her edgy. When Catherine ran out the door to catch the school bus, Lindsey gathered Christopher in her arms, going almost at a run herself to her old battered station wagon. Only, as Lindsey flung the door to her house shut behind her, she stopped incredulously to look at the spot in her drive where her old Ford should have been parked.

There, instead of finding her familiar vehicle where she had left it, she saw a shining new station wagon. It had a huge red ribbon wrapped around its gleaming gray exterior, topped by a gigantic bow. A quick sweep of her darkening eyes told her that her own car was nowhere in sight.

Several of her neighbors were already out studying the new station wagon, and they watched her obviously startled reaction gleefully, knowing smiles on their faces. Aghast, Lindsey walked slowly to the new car.

"Got a secret friend, Lindsey?"

"Open it, Mrs. Wiltse!"

"Go on, get in."

She barely heard the encouraging, laughing words. Someone came and took Christopher out of her arms, while another gawker slipped the oversized ribbon up and out of the way of the car door.

Lindsey opened the driver's door unwillingly. She had needed a new car for so long, and this one was beautiful. The upholstery was a deep blue, in a luxuriant, plush fabric. The surrounding vinyl molding was a smoky gray, matching the car's exterior. In the backseat there was a new child carrier, replacing the frayed and torn one Christopher had used since he was an infant. The keys were in the ignition.

Lindsey breathed in the smell of newness: fabric and metal and plastic all blending to make an aroma that was labeled comfort and dependability. Absently she brushed her hand across the back of the driver's seat.

The owner's papers were on the passenger side. Dazedly Lindsey picked them up and thumbed through them. Insurance papers were included, needing only her signature. With unsteady fingers Lindsey grasped the last item: a small, white envelope not unlike the one that had accompanied the roses. A deep breath, an agonizing pause, and she ripped it open.

The gas tank is full, Lindsey Wiltse, was written in an arrogant, masculine scrawl. *Enjoy.* The signature read simply, *J.* Then, as a postscript: *I thought the color matched your eyes.*

Lindsey let the note flutter downward to rest on the plush blue upholstery. Jeremy really knew how to twist a screw, she thought bitterly. How she wished she could tell him exactly what she thought of him. A cold wrath overwhelmed the beginnings of desire she had felt to actually own this car. She would not drive it. She dared not.

Her expression black, Lindsey slammed the door shut. She knew her neighbors were awaiting her reaction to finding the new car in her driveway. With a grim smile, she remembered what she had done with Jeremy's roses. She wished frustratedly that she could dump the shining gray automobile into some garbage heap.

Storming silently, she took Christopher out of her neighbor's arms. Uncompromisingly she stood, holding Christopher, her back ramrod straight, her cheeks flushed, her eyes overbright, surveying the audience that had gathered.

"There has been some mistake," she said with a calmness she did not feel. "The car was not meant for me at all." Then, disregarding the unbelieving stares and open speculation in her neighbors' faces, Lindsey swung away from the object of her anger and stalked back to her front door.

She knew better than to try to return the car. She was sure Jeremy would have left the dealership explicit instructions regarding any attempt she might make to do so. How she despised him. Did he think he could soften her up by buying her?

No, she could not be bought, and neither would she be intimidated. She discovered, to her dismay, that she was trembling, but she told herself it was nothing that a face-to-face encounter with Jeremy Boulanger would not cure. In the meantime, if she could do nothing about the automobile parked in her driveway, she at least could refuse to drive it.

Still holding Christopher, Lindsey reached for her telephone book. It took only a minute to find what she was looking for.

"Taxi?" she asked. "Yes…1568 Marlow Terrace, please. And hurry, I'm terribly late for work. What? Oh yes, it was car trouble all right."

"Mommy?" Christopher spoke for the first time. "Can't we keep the new car? I think it's pretty."

"No, we can't," she said shortly, straightening his hat. "And I don't want to hear another word about it, okay?"

At four-thirty Lindsey was cleaning off her desk in preparation for the weekend ahead, when her phone rang demandingly. She picked it up quickly, answering with her usual calm, businesslike voice. "Lindsey Wiltse here."

An unmistakable male drawl greeted her. "Good afternoon, Mrs. Wiltse."

How confident he sounded. Lindsey's fingers tightened around the receiver as she fought the impulse to hang up on him again. She forced herself to remain cool.

"Who is speaking, please?"

There was a slight pause. "Well done, Lindsey," he congratulated, amusement rich in his voice. When she remained silent, he continued, "Dinner tomorrow night, Mrs. Wiltse?"

She knew he was making good his promise that she would go out with him. Her mind racing, Lindsey searched for words with which to salvage her pride.

"I'm sorry," she managed with freezing politeness. "I would like to speak with you, but I'm afraid dinner is out. Perhaps you could meet me at my office at, say, eight-thirty Monday morning?"

"No deal, Lindsey. Either you go out to dinner with me, or I just keep doing what I have been doing."

"Perhaps I like it," she tried.

"Not if you are the same Lindsey Wiltse I spoke to last week, you don't."

She felt her temper begin to rise. "You have no right to interfere in my life," she snapped.

"Dinner, Lindsey." He sounded slightly bored. "And your life certainly could use some interference, couldn't it?" His voice was pure silk.

Her nerves were stretched so tight that she was breathing in shallow gasps. With her free hand she pounded her desk helplessly. But she knew she must talk with him, get him to stop paying her bills. And she had to get her own car back. She held the telephone receiver as far away from her as she could reach while she tried to take deep, calming breaths.

"All right, Mr. Boulanger." Her voice, when at last she trusted it, was coldly sarcastic. "You win this round. I'll go to dinner with you."

"Eight o'clock Saturday night, then, Mrs. Wiltse." Jeremy sounded completely unperturbed by her anger. "That will give you time to put the wee ones in bed."

She knew he was laughing at her. She could imagine his face, arrogantly triumphant.

"Lindsey?" he demanded.

"All right," she repeated, finding she could barely get the words out. "I'll go with you...as I said...on Saturday night." The taste of defeat was so bitter she thought she might be sick. But it was only temporary, she convinced herself. Losing a battle was all right, as long as you won the war.

Lindsey slammed down the phone once he'd said goodbye, and again considered the money Jeremy had spent on her behalf. He was bound to use it as a lever against her. She snorted lightly. All her wits and intelligence were no weapon at all against the powerful force of hard cash. She would have to prove to him that she did not need what he was handing out. And in order to do that...

Feeling her face begin to redden, Lindsey picked up her phone to call Robert Connor, hoping against hope that he was in town.

Her teenage baby-sitter had been there fifteen minutes and Lindsey was just kissing Catherine good night when the doorbell rang. As per instructions, the sitter answered the summons. In the small house the voices carried clearly to Catherine's room.

"Is Mrs. Wiltse here?" Was it possible that there was a slight hesitancy in Jeremy's cold voice, as if he had expected to find her gone, was even now wondering if she were home?

"Yes..." The sitter was just beginning to answer when Lindsey swept into the living room, where Jeremy was standing like a caged bear, shrinking the room and absolutely intimidating Wendy, the sitter, who was already

making cow eyes at this vision of male handsomeness and
self-confidence who had come calling for her employer.

Jeremy's eyes flicked to Lindsey with something like relief, then they narrowed. His blue gaze traveled down the
length of her body and leisurely up again to her face, and a
corner of his mouth lifted slightly. Lindsey's demure, modest, lightweight gray suit, with its white silk ruffled blouse
that buttoned almost to her chin, was her only formal business attire. The straight, no-nonsense skirt hung well below
her knees. Conservative black pumps and a black business
bag completed her outfit. She wore no jewelry except her
wide gold wedding band, no makeup except the very light-
est touch of lip gloss and mascara, and she had pulled her
hair back tightly into a smooth, shining chignon.

Even as Jeremy's eyes were studying her, she openly returned his scrutiny. He wore a fine wool cream-colored
sweater pulled over a blue shirt, silk like her own. The form-
fitting slacks sheathed his well-muscled legs in a way that
could only be custom-made. When she felt his eyes resting
on her face, she deliberately took a few more seconds to
study him before she lifted her eyes to meet his. She lifted an
eyebrow in a deliberate parody of his own expression.

"Satisfied?" he asked, amused.

"You're really quite handsome for a snake," she replied
evenly. His eyes flashed at her, then left her face to rest on
something behind her.

"Who do we have here?" he asked softly, as Christopher
limped into the living room. Lindsey whirled, dropping her
defiant pose with her handbag, and went to kneel beside her
son. "What is it, Christopher?" she asked, as he took one
last step toward her.

"You forgot to kiss me good night, Mommy," he said
quietly, looking at her with the absolute trust of the young,
positive that she would not hesitate to meet this very important need before she left. Then his eyes swept up to look

at Jeremy, who had moved to stand beside the mother and son.

"Who is that man, Mommy?"

Lindsey turned her face up to Jeremy. *This one is innocent,* she challenged silently. *Be kind to him or I will...* But she did not have to finish the thought, because Jeremy had bent his long legs to crouch beside them. "My name is Jeremy Boulanger, son. I'm—" his gaze slid mockingly to meet hers, "—a friend of your mother."

"Okay," Christopher accepted. "Are you going to kiss me good night, Mommy?" Then, unbelievably, "Can he come kiss me, too?"

Cursing the fates that had made her forget Christopher when she had heard Jeremy's voice at the door, Lindsey shrugged helplessly. Jeremy rose with ease, then reached down to help pull her up by grasping her elbow. "Lead the way," he whispered in her ear.

So it was that Jeremy stood behind Lindsey as she tucked Christopher into his bed, careful to wrap his legs so that they would not be chilled in the night, watching as she tenderly kissed her son good-night. And then she had to stand by, her hands balled into tight fists at her side, when Christopher raised accepting arms to Jeremy, fully expecting him to kiss him good-night also. Jeremy obliged, his hand cupping the small boy's face gently. "Good night, Christopher," he said gently. "I'll bring your mother back safe and sound for you."

Lindsey felt her insides splinter. If it weren't for this man's father, Christopher and Catherine would have had a loving grandfather and grandmother to spoil them, to help her. She felt her heart harden along with her face, and she turned abruptly away, unwilling to let Christopher see the loathing she was sure was written there.

"Shall we go, Lindsey?" she heard Jeremy ask as he once again took possession of her elbow. As soon as they were clear of Christopher's room she jerked herself out of his grasp. "Don't touch me," she hissed, "you viper."

"Don't be predictable, Lindsey," he answered, but he did not try to touch her again.

Shrugging into her coat, she gave Wendy last-minute instructions, adding, "I will be home by ten-thirty, or earlier," for Jeremy's benefit. She wanted him to know she did not expect to be out long, that this was no pleasure date, for her. She knew he had gotten the message when she turned to him at last and saw the fire burning in his eyes once more. "If you're quite ready?" she said stiffly. He inclined his head and opened the door.

In order to get to the Porsche, they had to pass the new gray wagon. Its bright ribbon was hanging limply, part of its brilliant color dragging on the ground. Jeremy's sardonic gaze met hers, but it was not until the Porsche was purring smoothly down the highway that he spoke.

"The Trillium okay? I thought we could do a little dancing."

She sucked in her breath sharply. "I don't want to dance with you, and anyway, I'm not dressed for it," she said crossly.

He flicked an amused glance over her. "That's for sure," he said softly. "Do I really make you feel that insecure, Lindsey?"

She refused to answer, staring stiffly out the car window at the lights of the city outside. When he didn't comment further, she turned to him, her expression controlled, calm and set. "Look, Mr. Boulanger," she said in her best professional voice, "I don't know how you're used to dealing with people, but if this is an example of your usual behavior, I'm surprised someone hasn't sent you off to Dale Carnegie, or something."

He smiled briefly, but the smile didn't reach his eyes. His foot pressed hard on the accelerator and the sports car began to swerve around the curves in the highway that would take them to the restaurant he had mentioned.

"Hey," Lindsey said sharply, as they sped with what seemed to her reckless danger around a snow-covered curve, "you told Christopher you would bring me home safely, not make him an orphan."

Jeremy slowed down then, and the rest of the journey was passed in silence. Lindsey rested her hands on her lap, willed her body to relax and assumed what she hoped was a serene, untroubled expression. She thought about the day's activities, she thought about what she was going to do tomorrow, she even recited what she knew of the Declaration of Independence (fitting, she told herself), anything to keep her mind off the brooding man who was sitting close to her in the confines of the silver Porsche.

When they arrived at the exclusive restaurant, Lindsey was not surprised to see that they had been given what had to be the most secluded table in the room. The band would not start until another hour, and for a while the little alcove with three windows overlooking the Grand Traverse Bay gave the impression of intimate privacy. The room, darkened for atmosphere, heightened the effect, and as Lindsey looked across the candlelit table, she could not help but notice how the planes of Jeremy's face were emphasized in the shadowy light.

"Do you know what you would like?" Jeremy asked, studying the menu.

"No," Lindsey answered evenly. "Actually, I'm not really hungry. Perhaps I could have just a salad and some coffee." She knew there was no way she could eat with the thousands of butterflies that were fluttering in her stomach.

Jeremy looked at her with brooding eyes, his gaze lingering on her lips, before he said, "I will order dinner for you. You can eat as little of it as you wish. Perhaps you will surprise yourself and find you are quite hungry, after all."

She shrugged, not trusting herself to speak civilly. The evening was becoming more and more difficult. But when the waitress came and Jeremy ordered one of the more expensive wines on the list, she felt compelled to speak. "No," she said abruptly, causing both Jeremy's and the waitress' eyes to swing in her direction. "None for me, that is...I mean, I never drink, and..." She took a deep breath, knowing she sounded more defensive than ever. "I never drive with people who drink. So if you don't want me to take a taxi home, you'd better not have anything either."

Oh, this is all so silly, she thought to herself. What has this man done to me? She felt like such a child. But all Jeremy did was say calmly, "All right, no wine. We will have soft drinks instead."

The waitress directed a sympathetic glance at him, but he ignored it and waited until she had gone before directing his next question at Lindsey. "You have religious beliefs that prohibit drinking?"

"No," she answered, feeling a flush steal up her face. "I just don't, that's all." This subject was too personal, but she could think of nothing to change it.

"Have you never drunk spirits?"

"Oh, please," she said. "What's the big deal? Of course I have. Now I don't. I haven't for a long time. What's so exceptional about not wanting any wine with dinner?"

"All right," he replied. "We will talk of something else. For instance, your mother's death. How old were you when she died?"

Silence. How dare he? *How dare he?* Sitting there so calmly, as if to talk of her most private wounds with a stranger, a Boulanger stranger, were an ordinary event. She turned her face away, looking blankly out the window at the lighted snowscape beyond.

"They were drunk, weren't they?" his voice was soft, measured. "Is that why you don't drink now?"

She expelled her breath in a hiss, unaware until that moment that she had been holding it. She turned back to him, furious emotion making her body rigid and her face pale. In her agitation she did not notice the waitress approaching with their food. She opened her mouth to speak, closed it, tried again.

Jeremy was watching her closely, but saved her from embarrassing herself as he said calmly, "Ah, here is our dinner. I admit to being famished myself, even if you are not hungry." She was silent as the plates were laid before them. Jeremy began to eat. Lindsey sat with hands folded on her lap, much as she had done in the car, staring out the window.

"Lindsey Wiltse, try to eat a little bit," he ordered softly. "You are much too thin. I imagine you often don't eat."

She looked at the succulent meat dish that had been placed before her, but her stomach was tied so tightly that she could not bring herself to even put a single bite in her mouth.

"Well, if you are not going to eat, and if you have nothing to say, I will make the necessary conversation," said Jeremy quite expressionlessly. "I did not want to come to Traverse City. After all, even though I look a lot like my father and that damns me in your eyes, I am not him, and I had absolutely no interest in coming here to meet you. And I am not surprised that you did not want to see me, either.

"But now that I have seen you, Lindsey Wiltse..."

She felt herself tremble at the way he said her name, for his tone was soft and full of seductive invitation.

"...I find myself quite attracted. No, wait," he continued as she made a small negative shake with her head. "You feel it, too, no matter how much you're trying to deny it. I didn't dream that kiss, Lindsey."

He pressed on. "There are simply some things that should be said. I was, after all, twenty years old when your mother died in that accident. I was older than you, and I saw things from a different perspective. That accident quite changed my father, you know.''

She flashed him a look of pure hatred. "It changed my father, too."

"Yes, well, I am sorry, but, damn it all, you have to understand that what happened years ago had nothing to do with me. I am here simply as an emissary. Why won't you let my father continue to help you, Lindsey? He wants to, you know. He knows you are in financial straits, and he has plenty of money."

"Guilt money," she interjected fiercely.

"Yes, guilt money, if you will," he answered curtly. "And what harm would it do to accept a little of it?"

"*No.*"

She looked away, resentment flaring. Nervously she twisted her wedding band around her finger. She did not think she had met anyone so determined as this dark man sitting opposite her, but she knew that somehow she must find the strength inside herself to withstand him and what he was offering.

Make a decision, she told her weakening brain. Take a course of action. He's a businessman. He'll understand logic. Argue with him.

"What you said the other day is true," she began. "What happened to my parents, everything surrounding their deaths, happened a long time ago." She took a deep breath and forced herself to continue. "You were right when you said that I should have outgrown my feelings about what happened, and frankly, I thought I had. But I never talk about what happened, not to anyone since Bradley died, and your father's letters, followed by your appearance, put me at a disadvantage. But—" she turned to face him for the first time since she had begun talking, her face a study in willful determination, "—the feelings are still there. I actually feel physically ill at the thought of taking money from John Boulanger. What would help me the most is for you to just go away. Go home. I was doing fine without you." She ignored the sardonic raise of an eyebrow in his closely shuttered face. "And I will do just fine when you are gone."

She reached into her handbag and pulled out a piece of paper with some figures listed in a precise row down one side of it. "Here," she said, shoving the paper across the table at him.

"What is this?" Jeremy asked sharply.

"It's obvious," she explained patiently. "That is the total, as near as I could figure it, of what you have spent on my behalf. And here—" now she slid a check across the pristine white tablecloth, "—is money to pay you back."

"Where did you get this?" His voice was harsh with surprise, his eyelids lowered so she could not read the expression in them.

"It does not matter. I did get it. The check is quite good, you can cash it tomorrow."

He shot out a hand to grab her wrist, tight. "Where did you get the money, Lindsey?" This time when she almost automatically twisted her wrist to free it, he was ready for her and merely tightened the pressure on the bones there.

"I am not destitute, I assure you," she told him haughtily. "But there is one more thing. I did not include money for the car. I want my car back. I want you to return the new one and give me mine back."

He let go of her hand, but made no move to pick up her check. "I do believe you mean it," he said slowly, almost disbelieving. "You would return everything."

"I told you I could not be bought," she said proudly.

He shrugged. "Most people can, at one price or another." His gaze raked her drawn, taut features. "You have a price, too, Lindsey Wiltse. I just haven't found it, yet."

"You are unforgivable."

"Maybe. Where did you get the money, Lindsey?"

"None of your business. I got it, that's all."

"Was it your blond truck driver, Lindsey?" With grim disapproval he watched the telltale blush sweep over her face. "And what did you have to give as collateral?"

Stop it, she screamed at him silently. Accepting help from Robert had been distasteful to her, but she had not known how much her pride had been hurt until she had glimpsed the raging scorn in Jeremy's eyes. She felt like crying, but she didn't want Jeremy Boulanger to know that. She felt empty, humiliated. She could not even dredge up the old hatred as a weapon against what this man was doing to her. She felt nothing, she felt empty, and she felt like crying, as if something precious had been lost to her forever. She wished Jeremy would take her home so she could sleep. She wished she could sleep for a month.

"My father wants to see you," Jeremy was saying, watching her face.

A negative shake was the only answer she would give him.

"He's dying. He wants to make his peace with you." Jeremy quoted his father's words to her.

"That's impossible," she threw back at him, finally finding her voice. "There can be no peace between him and me. If it will make him feel any better, just tell him that I hardly think about him anymore. My mother was a grown woman, she knew what she was doing. So did my father..." she choked, and tears swam before her eyes. "Excuse me." She stumbled to her feet, meaning to head to the lounge before she completely disgraced herself. "Please go back to your father, Mr. Boulanger," she said finally, willing her voice to be calm, even as the tears started to fall down her cheeks. "Tell him I'm flattered I rated enough importance in his life that he sent you. But please tell him that I want nothing of the name Boulanger, ever again."

It was a great exit line, and would have been effective if her voice had not been swimming with grief, and if Jeremy had not also risen to come around to her seat, had not put his hands on her shoulders and pushed her down into her chair. He seemed oblivious to any attention that they were causing, and really, the seating was so private, they were not causing very much.

"Sit down, Mrs. Wiltse," he said quietly. He left his hands on her shoulders in a gentle embrace, and she found she did not have the strength to shake him off. For a few endless moments he left his hands there, unmoving, against her jacket. Then with a sigh he lifted his hands to let them rest on her head. She felt him begin to remove the pins from her smooth chignon.

"What are you doing?" she gasped.

"Taking your hair down," he replied calmly. "I've been wanting to do it all evening."

Through clenched teeth she said tightly, "I gave you no permission to touch me."

"I didn't ask, Lindsey," he responded. As her hair fell in soft waves around her shoulders, Jeremy began to run his fingers through it, massaging her temples lightly. She felt his hands move over her scalp, she felt his knuckles brush her jawline gently.

"Stop it," Lindsey pleaded, even as he pulled her head back slightly so that it rested against his soft wool sweater. She could feel the taut muscles of his stomach against the back of her head.

"I'm not hurting you, Lindsey," he said. "I won't hurt you anymore. My father and I have been such bastards. Let me make it up to you. Just let me touch you for a minute. It's what you need."

Damn him for being so knowledgeable. Lindsey was finding it more and more difficult to breathe. No one had touched her in such a caring, intimate way since Bradley had died. She began to feel a tightness in her abdomen, a yearning that was at odds with the anger she should be feeling.

Where was the waitress? When would he stop?

She was so overwhelmingly tired. Just for a minute she would rest, and then she would begin the fight all over again. In the meantime, Jeremy's hands massaged her head, her temples; they rubbed softly against her cheeks, her jaw-line, then lowered to massage her shoulders.

Through an almost semiconscious daze Lindsey felt Jeremy tug at her suit jacket. "Take this off, Lindsey," he commanded softly, and she offered no protest when he lifted it off her. Once again he began that oh-so-seductive massage of her shoulders, up her neckline, down again, dipping his fingers in front to the swell of her breasts. Her lips parted, and she relaxed more completely against him. She heard the ragged breathing that signaled his own arousal.

What are you doing, Lindsey? an inner voice mocked. You let him get past your defenses, that's for sure. Sit up, get out of his reach, *now. Sit up, Lindsey.* The inner voice was screaming by the time she was able to heed it, and she struggled against her haze of tiredness, weakness and sheer pleasure, to shake Jeremy's hands off. When he realized she was offering resistance, he paused, and she thought he might speak, but instead he left her at last to regain his seat opposite the table from her. She bit her lip to keep from crying aloud at the loss of his touch. His eyes were darkened pools of blue-black desire, and she stared at him, her own expression a mixture of hunger and anguish. Her mouth trembled with the force of her need; she saw his gaze fix intently on her parted lips.

She could not help it. No longer caring who spoke first or who was in control, she spoke, trying to break this tension that had sprung between them.

"I do want my car back." Her voice sounded hoarse, husky.

He stiffened. "Your car—" he paused slightly for emphasis, "—is sitting in the driveway of your home."

"And I want you to quit paying my bills...." She went on as if he had never spoken.

"So lover boy can take over?" he asked quietly.

"And I want you to get the hell out of my life."

"No."

A single word, but said with much more authority than she had managed when she threw it at him.

Her response was bitter. "You are true Boulanger, through and through, Jeremy, no matter what you think. You look like him, you act like him. He has trained you well." She knew she had gotten through to him at last by the tightening of his mouth, by the cold iciness replacing the hot desire in his eyes. Then his expression gentled. "Let's not argue, Lindsey Wiltse. The band has started. Dance with me?" He held out his hand.

It was ludicrous. She should refuse. She wanted to refuse. But something stronger, something more basic, the need to be touched again by those warm caring hands, to be held, if even for a minute, as if she were truly cherished, had her nodding a dazed assent. And Jeremy led her to the dance floor as the band swung into a romantic, melodic, slow tune.

Jeremy did not hesitate. He enfolded Lindsey in his arms as if she belonged nowhere else, pulling her to him, feeling her trembling slender form acquiesce to his embrace as they moved together in response to the music. And Lindsey, because she was so tired and disturbed, because she still hadn't eaten and felt weak as a result, because it had been so long since anyone had stormed her defenses, and because it just felt so right, found herself lifting her arms to encircle Jeremy's neck. Jeremy's eyebrows shot up, then his gaze grew tender as his arms tightened around Lindsey.

"I know what you're thinking," she muttered against his sweater. "But it's not true. You haven't won, or anything."

He laughed into her ear, his breath warm against her. "That wasn't what I was thinking at all. Would you like to know what I was thinking?"

She nodded dreamily.

"I was thinking that if you can't get her drunk, Jeremy old boy, you can at least get her tired." His right hand began a light massage from hip to shoulder, feeling her body melt against him. "You are tired, aren't you Lindsey? Tired and thin and brave and tough and angry and—" she felt his lips graze her temple, "—beautiful. So beautiful. My beautiful Lindsey Wiltse." He held her to him when she would have pulled away. "Relax, Lindsey. Forget my name is Boulanger, just for a little while. Enjoy yourself. You deserve it."

And surprisingly she wanted to do just that. She was tired of fighting, tired of being defensive, tired of being alone, and right now her body was sending her messages she thought it had long ago forgotten. It felt wonderful to be held so securely, even if the arms surrounding her belonged to the enemy. Only he didn't feel like the enemy, not anymore. She realized he was talking again.

"Say my name, Lindsey," he directed.

"Boulanger," she responded hazily.

"No." His voice deepened. "Jeremy. Say it. I want to hear you say it when you're not angry or resentful." When she didn't respond he shook her. "Say Jeremy."

"Jeremy." It was little more than a sigh, and she was asleep, standing in the circle of his arms, her head against his chest, while the music played on.

Chapter Five

Lindsey woke slowly, lazily. She could not remember when she had slept so soundly, with so little interruption. She stretched languidly, noting groggily that she was dressed in only her underwear. She stopped in mid-stretch, her arms raised above her head, her legs pulled taut. She always slept with a nightdress. Surely she was not so tired last night that she forgot to put anything on to sleep in.

Last night... She lowered her arms and shook her head into wakefulness. The truth was that she simply could not remember the end of the evening. She was sure that she and Jeremy had danced, but she could remember little else through the thick haze that was her memory. More clearly she recalled her uneaten dinner, the conversation bandied back and forth between Jeremy and herself, the unbelievable gentleness of Jeremy's hands.

But hard as she searched, there was no image, no memory of returning home, of seeing to the sitter, of preparing for bed. Now here she was lying in her bed in a most unusual fashion. Thoroughly confused, she looked around her room, which was bathed in sunlight. Sunlight? In a room that faced west? With a sense of impending doom she searched frantically for the clock-radio she had moved in from the kitchen. The digital figures glowed steadily: one-thirty-eight. One-thirty-eight? In the afternoon?

Abruptly Lindsey swung her feet around and down to the floor. Slowly she began to notice other details: her clothes of the night before were neatly folded over her desk chair; draped around them was a man's cream-colored sweater. Fully alert at last, she grabbed a robe out of her closet, slipped into it, belted it without bothering with the accompanying buttons, and sped out of her room.

"Catherine? Christopher?" she called, her voice unusually sharp in the waiting stillness.

Jeremy Boulanger's voice responded from her living room. "In here, Lindsey. All safe and sound."

With a low moan Lindsey leaned against the wall outside her room. What had happened? What was he doing here? Crossing her arms in front of her breasts, she tried to still her sudden trembling. Then, with a toss of her head and a raising of her chin, she strode into her living room.

Jeremy's long, trim body was sprawled comfortably on her earth-toned sofa. His legs were stretched out so that his feet could rest on the sturdy, well-worn coffee table that Bradley had made from old barn wood long ago. Dressed in the same silk shirt and tailored slacks that he had worn last night, Jeremy had a child seated on either side of him. She stared at him in consternation as he continued reading to her children from a favorite book of stories and poems. A pillow and blanket, usually kept stored in her hall cupboard, were stacked neatly at one end of the sofa.

Jeremy paused in his reading long enough to direct a bland look of inquiry at Lindsey. "Good morning," he finally offered, his tone deceptively mild. "Or should I say, good afternoon?"

A seemingly bottomless hatred glittered savagely in her gray eyes as she gazed at him. Her heart pounded erratically in her chest.

"Now that your mother is up, we can quit whispering," he said to Catherine and Christopher, but his eyes remained glued to hers. His intimately suggestive perusal was roaming over her features, and a dark challenge glittered from his brooding eyes. Then, deliberately, he turned from her to give his full attention to her son and daughter. "And do you know what that big lion said?" he asked dramatically.

Christopher shook his head, enchanted. Catherine grinned spontaneously, and Lindsey could see that her daughter was so caught up in the suspense of Jeremy's story that she was actually holding her breath.

"ROAAAAAARRRRR" Jeremy uttered the word with such a loud, mock-ferocious voice that Lindsey gave a little gasp herself. "And then..." he continued.

She found her voice at last.

"Mr. Boulanger..."

"Jeremy," he instantly corrected, winking at Christopher.

"Mr. Boulanger," she repeated, distinctly emphasizing each syllable. "What are you doing here?"

"Well," he drawled, eyeing her faded purple housecoat with its giant pink flowers dubiously. "Maybe after you get dressed, we can talk about it." His blue eyes glinted at her with amusement. "In the meantime, Catherine and Christopher and I will finish our story."

"Oh," she said with exasperation.

"Don't bother putting your hair up, though," he continued, laughter lacing his voice. "I much prefer it as it is right now than the way you wore it last night."

"I couldn't care less what you prefer and what you don't prefer," she shot at him. "My only interest is getting you out of my house."

"Not until we talk, Lindsey," he said with exaggerated patience. "Now be a good girl and go get dressed so that we—" his arms went around Catherine and Christopher in a spontaneous hug, "—can continue undisturbed."

Lindsey wondered frantically if she could move; she was trembling uncontrollably in her anger. Finally making a decision, she turned on her heel and stalked back to her bedroom. There, behind her closed door, she stood and took ten deep breaths, fighting for self-control.

She saw again in her mind's eye that incriminating blanket and pillow on her sofa, announcing to anyone who cared to look that he had spent the night. How dared he? *How dared he?*

She turned and caught sight of herself in her own dresser mirror. Her auburn hair was spread wildly around her face, her eyes were wide, flashing angry sparks, her cheeks were flushed. But the sight that caught and held her eyes was her robe, wrapped and belted so hurriedly just a few minutes earlier, gaping open to her waist.

"Ooooooh," Lindsey moaned, sitting abruptly on her bed. Tears pricked her eyelids, and her shoulders slumped. Never could she remember feeling such helpless anger.

Slowly she rose from her bed. So he had spent the morning baby-sitting Catherine and Christopher, had he? Well, let him baby-sit a little longer while she assembled her own arsenal. She pulled on old jeans that used to fit her like a second skin, and even now didn't hang too badly on her slender form. A crisp white blouse and a blue blazer completed her outfit.

When she moved to the bathroom she was met by the sight of his maroon shaving kit taking up space on her vanity. Fury swelled like a wave. Jeremy Boulanger had gone too far this time, much too far. Again, she deliberately slowed her breathing. As she went through the motions of her morning ablutions, her mind remained fixed on one murderous thought: *He'll pay for this. I'll make him pay.*

It was only as she brushed out her hair that her body stilled and she remembered how, last night, his hands had loosened her chignon, how he had combed his fingers through her silken tresses, how he had massaged her neck and shoulders . . .

Stop it right now, she told herself sternly, looking at her image in the mirror. That's a fire too hot for you to play with. Jeremy Boulanger can have all the women he wants, so why would he want you? Seduction is a technique to him, it helps him get what he wants. After all, he's his father's son.

I'm not my father, he had argued last night, and she wished now that he was. She could have handled the father much more easily than the son. That's probably what John Boulanger was counting on, she told herself derisively. The old Boulanger charm, in the form of his son, should soften the lonely widow. Well, he could just go charm the pants off of someone else, she would keep hers on, thank you.

Bradley, I need help. Why aren't you here? Why did you leave me to face this alone? I am so confused, and I am filled with hate.

Hate is wrong, self-destructive, Bradley had patiently explained. *You will not be completely healed until you learn to forgive.*

I can't forgive, she shouted. *He stole my mother and killed my father. I will hate him forever and forever.*

She looked at her right hand. It was gripping her hairbrush with abnormal ferocity. Her knuckles glowed white against its black handle.

She dropped the brush onto her Formica counter. Her forefinger traced the stitching of Jeremy's shaving kit, noticing for the first time that the deep purple material was fine dyed leather.

The violence of her raging emotions trembled through her, stiffening every sinew into finely tempered steel.

Thrusting aside Bradley's memory, she went marching out to meet the enemy.

She found him quietly resting, his eyes closed, his head laid back against the arch of her sofa. The children's book was on the seat beside him, his arms were folded against his chest. Catherine and Christopher had abandoned him only so far as to play with some Legos on the floor at his feet. He looked completely relaxed, his face such a mask of bland innocence that she was sure he was awake. So she was not surprised when Jeremy cocked one eye open to study her, standing, once again, in the doorway of her own living room. And, once again, she was subject to that maddeningly lazy perusal.

"You," she said coldly, "have a lot of explaining to do."

He grinned then, a completely unself-conscious, boyish grin, and it was almost her undoing.

Remember who he is, she told herself sternly. Remember who you are. Don't be taken in by a smile full of white teeth, for heaven's sake. Get a hold of yourself.

He untangled his legs and stood up, watching her carefully. "There are few things I'd enjoy more than having a normal conversation with you, Lindsey Wiltse," he said, "but first I think you'd better have something to eat, hmm?" He smiled crookedly as she glared at him. "Come on, Lindsey, I've been known to make a mean omelet in my time, and your refrigerator has all the fixings." She gaped at him. "Well, don't just stand there. Come on." He took her hand and led her into the kitchen.

"I don't want you to fix me anything," she said with deadly emphasis. "All I want is—"

"Tut, tut, Lindsey. Not even a thank you for what I believe to be the first really good sleep you've had in a long time? And I was such a perfect gentleman, too, spending the night on that horribly lumpy sofa, all the time dreaming of the delectable body I found when I undressed—"

"That's enough!" she said crushingly.

"That's my girl." He smiled again.

"I am not your girl!" she exploded in boiling wrath.

Catherine wandered into the kitchen just in time to hear her mother's fierce words. "Mommy's not a girl," she said importantly.

"No, I can see that," Jeremy agreed. He flicked a burning glance over her, in that one look stripping away her clothes and making her feel naked.

"Are you going to make Mommy breakfast, too?" Catherine asked with the breezy unawareness of youth.

"Well, yes, if I can persuade her to sit long enough to eat it," Jeremy assured the little girl.

Catherine turned to her mother. "Jeremy cooks delicious things," she offered enthusiastically.

Biting her lip, Lindsey sat down with a thump on one of her plain, wooden kitchen chairs. She had the crazy impression that her life was careening out of control, and wondered why a simple no would not suffice for this insufferable man. She watched stonily while he gathered some eggs and cheese from her refrigerator. Embarrassingly, her stomach rumbled as the smells of cooking began to fill her kitchen.

"How long has it been since you've eaten?" Jeremy asked, not turning from the stove.

"Yesterday lunch," she answered resentfully.

"What did you have then?"

"Oh, enough," she evaded.

He turned and looked at her, his one eyebrow cocked in the expression she was beginning to know so well. His voice was calm, but she sensed the steely determination underneath. "And what was enough, Lindsey?"

She considered a lie, then rejected it in favor of the harmless truth. "A chocolate bar and a cup of coffee," she admitted tersely.

He put the perfectly cooked omelet on a plate in front of her, then poured a cup of steaming coffee. Toast and orange juice followed. "No wonder you collapsed on me last night," he said evenly. She looked at him sharply to see if he was mocking her, but she could detect nothing at all in his eyes. She colored and glanced away.

"Why couldn't you eat last night, Lindsey? I thought you were just being stubborn."

"I was, I suppose," she blurted out. "That is, I meant to eat before you picked me up but time got away from me and—"

"You couldn't bear to eat in my presence," he finished for her. Again his voice was calm, but she sensed anger underneath.

"You needn't sound so insulted," she retorted. "I always have a hard time eating when I'm tense." She shrugged unconcernedly. "I'm surprised I don't have ulcers, or something."

He raked her slender figure with his eyes. "You must be tense a lot, Lindsey Wiltse."

She picked up the coffee he had prepared for her and sipped it. She sat, her eyes gazing straight ahead at her yellow kitchen wall, refusing to acknowledge his concern, or lack of it.

She felt rather than heard his sigh. He pulled out a chair across from her and sat down, moving himself directly into her line of vision. She stared at him blankly.

When he spoke, his voice was calm and deep. "Listen, Lindsey. I find myself being truly sorry that we had to meet under such inauspicious circumstances. I know you feel that I've given you a lot of grief, and I apologize. But I'll be hanged if I'll accept all that resentment and pride from you because of something my father did fifteen years go. Besides, Lindsey, he's changed. Give the man some credit, for heaven's sake. He loved Ruth Ann, and could hardly function for over a year after her death. He has his scars."

"Bully," she said.

His eyes grew dark, angry, piercing. "Haven't you an ounce of forgiveness or compassion in your body?" he demanded. "When did you become judge and jury for the sins of the world?"

"Not the world. Only John Boulanger."

He stood, scraping the chair noisily against the floor, and turned his back to her.

"Well," she said defensively. "How did you feel about the accident, when it happened?"

He took the few steps that led him to the sink, shoving his hands into his pockets. He stood watching an early robin outside her kitchen window. "I was merely an observer. My father and I have never been...close. I think Ruth Ann was the only person he has ever really cared about."

His few words taught her more than she wanted to know. He had been lonely, she thought unwillingly. As a boy he had wanted his father to love him. Perhaps they had something in common, after all.

She felt the betraying tears close in on her. *Hate-love. Judgment-compassion. Friend-enemy.* Life's opposites filled her with dizzy confusion. Where she sought clarity, she saw only choices. Where she felt hatred, love stood grieving right around the corner. When she decided to act, other options continued to haunt her.

Impulsively Lindsey began explaining to Jeremy how she felt. "I'm sorry," she began. "I've given you a one-sided impression, and it's quite the wrong one. I am trying so hard not to hate your father."

She paused, took a deep breath, then forced an air of indifference into her voice as she continued. "I think that the human condition, life itself, places no limits on what we can achieve, or on what we can suffer. I have thought about your father and my mother thousands of times. They were adult people making adult choices. I can accept that. What I can't do is make the hurt go away. I'm twenty-seven years old, and it still hurts, and I still want to hurt back. I don't want to hate, but I can't seem to help it. So, you see, I really can't handle John Boulanger wanting to make amends now, after so many years. I just want him to leave me alone.''

"I never thought you were a coward." Jeremy let a touch of sarcasm edge his voice.

"Coward?" she exclaimed in a low, furious voice. "Is that what you think? Your father cost me my parents, my childhood, practically my life! I'll admit I was very juvenile in the way I handled things, but then I was a juvenile at the time. My own guilt for being so unforgiving toward my mother, and then never having a chance to make it up later in life was devastating. Of course," she added caustically, "my father's suicide didn't help."

"His what?" Jeremy whirled toward her.

"You mean you didn't know?" She sipped her coffee, striving to remain cool. "I would have thought you would have known that, considering all the other things you know about me."

"No," Jeremy answered grimly. "I didn't know."

Lindsey rose, walked as far from Jeremy as she could get in her small kitchen to lean against her back door.

How is it she was not over this? she thought wearily. It was done with years ago.

"Well, he did," she said finally. "Within a year of the accident. In the pickup, in the garage, while I was at school. I was...the one who found him." Through a haze of newly remembered grief she felt Jeremy's hands on her shoulders, pulling her tightly coiled body against his own. She went to him, unresisting.

"What happened to you then?"

"The usual." She gave a little hiccuping laugh. "I had no relatives, so I became a ward of the state. Only I...I..." She gave a great shudder and began to cry in earnest.

She did not struggle when Jeremy turned her, and with the palm of his hand pressed her head into his shoulder. How long she stood here, crying huge racking sobs while he held and caressed her, she did not know, but she did know that when at last her sobs tapered off to controllable sniffles she realized that his shirt was soaked with her tears.

Embarrassed, she attempted to put some distance between them by putting her hands on his chest to push him away. But he would not allow it, folding her hands gently between them. He tightened his arms around her once more. "Tell me," he commanded. "Tell me what happened to you."

And she realized that she really did want to tell him, to explain that which had never fully been admitted, not even to Bradley. But not like this, all wet and clingy in his arms.

"All right," she said. "Only let me sit down. I'm all right now. I'm sorry. I can't think what happened to me. I don't usually fall apart like that. I suppose I ought to thank you."

"Right," he said. "Sure. You must be filled with gratitude for me and mine." She looked at him, startled, surprised at the bitterness in his tone. But he was smiling now, a soft, tender smile that took her breath away.

"Your breakfast is cold, Lindsey."

"I'll just heat it up again in the microwave," she said. "I'll eat it. I really do feel hungry." She grinned. "After a certain hunger point is reached, anything tastes good, even reheated omelets."

"While you're doing that, I'll look in on the children," Jeremy stated. "I have a feeling this may take awhile."

He returned just as she was sitting down with her newly warmed omelet. "I promised Catherine and Christopher a special treat if they would play quietly while we talked," he explained, as he poured himself a cup of coffee and sat across the table from Lindsey. "Now, tell me what happened to you, Lindsey Wiltse."

And she did. She told him about the series of foster homes, some good, some terrible. She told him about the young girl who was so embittered she alienated everyone around her, and thus faced constant rejection. She told him about lying and stealing, until she was placed in a home for especially tough cases. She talked about the restrictions placed on the girls who lived there, how it had felt like a prison to her, how in spite of the tight rules she had run away, not once, but three times.

"Where did you go, when you ran away?" he prodded.

She paused, her face full of remembered pain and loneliness. "That was the problem. There was never anyplace. I always ended up back at the door, my hat in hand, asking to be let in."

Suddenly her recitation ceased, and her head went up proudly. "You've got pity in your eyes, Jeremy. Stop it right now. I came out all right. It was a tough school, but no tougher than others I have had to deal with."

"And Bradley?" he asked quietly, his eyes never leaving her face.

She looked down then, unable to meet the steadiness of his gaze.

"Yes, well, Bradley saved my life. First literally—the first time he saw me I was being attacked by some of the really tough kids from school, and then emotionally—he got me to graduate at that high school, much as I hated it. He stood by me and just cared, no matter what I did or how I acted. And then he married me."

"And do you still love him?" Jeremy's face seemed strangely tight, shuttered.

She considered her answer carefully. "Of course," she said slowly. "But I understand that he's dead. And that he wasn't perfect. That's important to understand: that you can love someone even when he's not perfect. I used to think that it diminished me to have loved so imperfect a person with so complete a love. But now I realize it didn't. Love given at any time is an enlarging experience."

She was talking more to herself than to Jeremy; it almost surprised her to find him still sitting across from her.

"Sometimes I feel as if he's here, in the room with me, trying to help me. Do you think that's crazy?"

"No," Jeremy answered steadily. "Nothing about you is crazy, Lindsey. You're refreshingly sane. Life has given you some bruising blows, and you have survived all of them. You're strong and brave and intelligent, not to mention being a truly excellent mother."

She felt her face go hot, looked down, and began to eat her twice-cooked omelet. The compliment unnerved her; she felt gauche, inexperienced.

"Thank you," Jeremy said softly.

"What?" she said blankly.

"The appropriate response after receiving a compliment is, thank you."

"Oh. Yes. Well, thank you." She continued eating, stubbornly refusing to look up to see the amusement she was sure to find on Jeremy's face.

"Are you done talking?" asked Catherine from the doorway. Christopher was standing beside her.

It was Jeremy that answered. "Yes, I think we are, children," he said easily. "And when your mother is finished eating, we'll think of some special things to do with you."

"Promised a treat," Christopher reminded, his baby blue eyes looking at Jeremy adoringly.

"So I did," Jeremy acknowledged. "And I think a very special treat is to go and get some ice cream."

"With you?" Catherine asked eagerly.

"And with your mother," Jeremy agreed, walking around to stand behind Lindsey's chair. He placed his hand on her shoulder; she sensed the possessiveness there, the new tenderness.

Stop him, she told herself. He is not what you want. You've told your story and now he feels he owns you.

She shrugged his hand off.

Still not looking at him, she said skeptically, "All four of us in your silver trinket?"

"No, Lindsey," he returned calmly. "We'll have to go in your car for us all to fit."

"I don't have a car." The bitter, defensive words were out before she could help herself.

"Well." She had made him angry, but he was exerting a firm control on his temper. "That station wagon out there belongs to one of us, at any rate," he said with cutting politeness. "You have the keys, and I had it gassed up. We will take it."

"Great!" exclaimed Catherine. "Mommy wouldn't even let us touch it before."

She finally looked at him, tilting her chin and straightening her shoulders, meeting his hooded look with a defiant one of her own.

"Would you deny your children their treat, Lindsey?" he asked with deceptive calm.

With an angry shrug she moved to get coats and hats out of the hall closet. "Oh, all right," she acquiesced sourly. "Just don't read more into this than there is, that's all."

"Of course not," he agreed casually. Too casually. If she had learned anything, it was that nothing Jeremy Boulanger ever did was casual.

A short time later they were comfortably ensconced in the new car. Christopher and Catherine sat with quiet good manners in the back seat, while Jeremy drove with smooth skill. Lindsey sat with her hands folded, wondering how she had allowed things to get this far. She was being undone by Jeremy's niceness. She had said yes to too many things; she was forgetting how to say no. Not that saying no did her any good, she admitted ruefully. So far not a single one of her demands had been met. This was a trend that had to stop.

"What is Jeremy's business, Mom?" Catherine's question interrupted her thoughts.

"What?" she asked, momentarily confused.

"Jeremy's business," Catherine repeated. "Like what Jeremy is here on."

She noticed Jeremy's hands tightening around the smoky gray steering wheel, felt him immediately tense at her side.

"Oh?" Catherine had her full attention now. "Did Jeremy tell you he was here on business?"

"No. He told Lucille that, didn't you, Jeremy?" Catherine's high girlish voice was happy, full of pride in what she had remembered. "You told your friend Lucille that you were in Michigan on business. That was why you had to miss your dinner date tonight."

"I see," Lindsey said coolly. Jeremy's face had gone quite expressionless.

"Yes," Catherine continued innocently. "He said it was taking longer than expected."

"Out of the mouths of babes . . ." Lindsey quipped. Jeremy's eyes sliced in her direction.

"Well, what is it?" Catherine demanded again.

"Business means work," Lindsey answered slowly. "Something you're paid to do. Something you would not do unless you were paid to do it. Right now, Jeremy's business is our family, or so he thinks."

Jeremy never said a word.

Lucille. He had called someone named Lucille. Was she his wife? Lover? In the short time she had known him it had never occurred to her that he might be married. Now that thought was like a knife in the heart.

Watch it, she told herself grimly. Your defenses are down. You've let him get too close. Get some distance, fast.

The only way to acquire that needed distance was to find out the nasty truth, and Lindsey determined to waste no time in doing so.

"Who *is* Lucille?" Lindsey asked acidly, after they had been served their ice cream. She and Jeremy were sitting in a cheerfully decorated red and white booth waiting for Catherine and Christopher to finish their tour of the western artifacts displayed charmingly in the Old West-styled parlor. "Is she your wife?"

Jeremy met her eyes steadily. "No."

"Lover then?"

"That is none of your business," he pointed out flatly.

"Oh, that word business again," she mocked with subtle irony. "I am your business, though, is that right? You know everything about me and my business, don't you? Well," she said conversationally, wiping strawberry ice cream off her upper lip with a paper napkin, "it seems highly unfair that you should know so much about my business and I should know nothing of yours."

His gaze narrowed on her in sharp question.

"Does Lucille know about my business, too?" she asked carelessly.

"No." His voice was cold, his face shuttered.

"Then she would hardly know about that business the other afternoon in my car, I dare say," she said mildly, taking another bite of ice cream.

Catherine and Christopher returned to the booth, their innocent faces alive with pleasure and wonder at the things they had seen. They made quick work of their sundaes, chattering and laughing happily with each other, unaware of the adult tension that surrounded them.

"Ready to go?" Jeremy asked when the children were finished.

"Eager to be rid of us, Mr. Boulanger?" Lindsey asked, her tone sugar-sweet.

He threw her a look of sheer annoyance. "I like your children, Lindsey," he said. "Unlike you, I have no desire to fight in front of them."

"Is that what we were doing?" She deliberately needled him. "I merely thought we were having a business discussion."

"It is time to go, Lindsey Wiltse," he said in total exasperation.

"Whatever you say, Mr. Boulanger," she murmured obediently, knowing that the barriers were back up between them, and that for the time being, she was safe.

When they arrived at Lindsey's home and had the children stripped of their winter clothing, Lindsey turned to Jeremy and held out her hand. "Thank you for everything," she said formally. "The children enjoyed their outing, and I appreciated the extra sleep. I know you must be in a hurry to have this business finished." She permitted herself a small, knowing smile. "And as you must realize by now, I am determined to remain independent. I trust you will accept the check I gave you last night as payment for... everything."

"I tore it up," he said with a careless shrug.

"I'll just have to write you a new one," she said implacably. "Then you can be on your way."

Jeremy took a single step toward her. "Why?" he taunted. "Your independence doesn't impress me, Lindsey, as much as your stupid prejudice and pride. You borrowed that money from Robert Connor, didn't you? What will your payment have to be for that debt?"

She blushed to the roots of her hair. "Nothing," she said in a low voice. "I promised him nothing."

His strong hand went out to grip her shoulder. "You didn't have to, Lindsey. The loan was promise enough. A man knows when not to press his advantage."

She turned away from him. "No," she answered evasively. "Robert is not like that." She glanced at him challengingly. "Don't judge all men by your standards, Jeremy."

She knew immediately that her words had been more powerful than she had intended, so furious did he become. His whole body went rigid, and his face was a mask of fierce anger.

Christopher, sensing at last the tension between the two adults, limped over to wrap his arms around Lindsey's legs.

"What's wrong?" he asked in his childish voice. "Jeremy mean?"

Jeremy's anger drained in an instant. Quickly he knelt down so that he could be eye level with Christopher. "No," he answered, "I'm not mean, Christopher. And to prove it, I'm going to play you a game of horse."

"Horse?" Christopher asked, his eyes round and questioning.

"Yes, horse. And this is the way you play. I get down on my hands and knees like this...and you get on my back like this...and we go galloping across the living room like this."

"Jeremy..." Lindsey began impatiently.

He looked up from where he was kneeling and winked at Lindsey. "Later," he said. "We'll talk about it later."

"There is nothing to discuss." She made her voice cold, which was more difficult than it should have been. It was suddenly very hard not to laugh, seeing Jeremy in his hand-tailored pants and silk shirt romping on her living room floor with Christopher on his back, while Catherine jumped up and down, clapping her hands excitedly. Whatever had possessed him to begin this noisy game? She tried to keep her own amusement from showing by remembering how angry she was, how the children would never settle for the night now, how he was causing her more problems by stirring them up to an unfamiliar gaiety.

But remembering all those things was a challenge, with her little house filled with the sounds of laughter such as it had never before known. Christopher had never known his own father, and Catherine knew him only as a dim memory. No wonder they were reacting to Jeremy as if he were their dream come true.

"Can Jeremy stay for dinner?" Catherine asked, pausing for a moment in her playful participation. "Please, Mommy."

Lindsey stood stock still in her living room that seemed no longer hers while he was there. He had taken over her house, he was taking over her children, and if she was not careful, he would take her over, too.

Jeremy was looking at her now from where he was playing with Christopher on the floor. Amusement was etched on his features as he waited for her response to Catherine's question, now repeated.

"Can he stay? Please?"

"I'm sure Mr. Boulanger has things he needs to do," she began gently, for her children's sake.

"I can't think of a single thing," he smiled blandly.

"And he needs to get back to Chicago," she continued as if he had not spoken.

"No hurry at all," Jeremy said. "I'm a true man of leisure." He gave Christopher another bounce, and the little boy squealed in delight. Jeremy cocked a brow at her. "That is, if it's not too much trouble for me to be here?"

She glared at him helplessly. "Oh, all right," she said ungraciously. "But we're not having anything special." She hated the mocking look that entered his eyes before he turned his attention to Christopher once more. "Be careful of Christopher's legs," she said sharply, then would have done anything to take her words back as Christopher's face, so ecstatic and wondering that this big man actually wanted to spend time with him, fell suddenly. Jeremy's eyes rebuked her callousness.

"Of course," he said, his voice low and gently reassuring. "I'll take very good care of Christopher."

"Oh," she said angrily, actually stamping her foot in her frustration. She whirled to go into her small kitchen. Couldn't he see what he was doing? What kind of man was he that he would lead her children on this way?

A man who likes children, the answer whispered itself into her mind, and her hands stilled over the food preparations.

Oh, go away, Jeremy Boulanger, she pleaded silently. *Go away soon. Please. While I can still resist you. Before you break my heart.*

Chapter Six

Dinner was over, Catherine and Christopher were bathed and kissed and tucked into bed. The little house was quiet, the children silent at last, in sleep.

Lindsey sat in the big, overstuffed easy chair, her arms crossed defensively over her breasts. Jeremy sat across from her on the sofa, one long, athletic leg casually crossed over the other. His hands were steepled in front of his chest.

"The time has come for us to reach some decisions." Jeremy's now familiar voice spoke with ominous calm.

Searing anger and resentment coursed through her veins. His relaxed air, his attitude of being completely in possession and command, was the igniting spark to her temper.

"You don't seem to understand, Jeremy Boulanger," she said with convincing emphasis. "All of my important decisions have been made, and they definitely do not include you. I want you out of my home. Now."

A faint, almost imperceptible nod was his acknowledgment of her words, and she had the familiar impression that he was playing with her, laughing at her. It put her back up.

She wondered if Jeremy ever allowed anyone else to have any power over him, to affect him in more than a superficial way. Without thinking, she gave voice to her silent questions. "You always need to be in control, don't you?" she challenged him.

His eyes narrowed as he asked in return, "What do you mean?"

"Well..." She took her time, trying to put into words the thoughts that had been niggling at the back of her consciousness since she had first met Jeremy Boulanger. She had his full attention now, and she moved her hands to rest gracefully on her lap as she tucked her bare feet under her and sat back.

"You're one of those people who thrives on power. Not just—" she waved her hand to encompass the invisible everything, "—money-type power." She threw him a look to see his reaction to her comments, and was not surprised to see a blank expression settle on his face. "I admit to a certain curiosity to see you at work, but what I'm talking about carries over to other things. You have to be in charge, or else you're uncomfortable. As I have no desire to allow you to be in charge of me, I must represent quite a challenge to you." The last sentence she said with an air of someone who has finally found the answer to an especially difficult riddle.

"I have always enjoyed challenges," he agreed blandly, but she could see that the light of battle was back in his eyes.

"As I said," she said lightly. "And you enjoyed today. However, I think you were a little surprised by how much you enjoyed it. It presented for you the perfect situation. I was the challenge." She actually had the nerve to throw him a wink. "And my children responded to your control. Of course, children the age of mine are easy to control and to... manipulate."

Jeremy uncrossed his legs, unsteepled his hands and leaned forward.

"I enjoyed your children, Lindsey," he bit out. "What you say may be true, but don't add Christopher and Catherine to your black list of my sins." He rose to look out her front window into the darkness outside.

"You have done a wonderful job with your children, Lindsey," he commented unexpectedly. "I have said so before. They are a delight."

Suddenly she was bereft of words. Underneath that calm, confident voice she was sure she had caught a touch of...longing, of wistfulness. The impression was wiped out as he continued forcefully. "They need a father, Lindsey. Christopher, especially, needs a man to pattern himself after."

"Are you applying for the position?" she asked, her voice husky, its tone unfriendly although couched in a polite phrase.

He swung around. "Is Robert Connor?"

It was sudden, this taking back of the reins of authority. It took her by surprise, and made her realize that she was truly a novice and had little chance of winning any verbal battles with this man. She looked at him standing against her darkened window, his face hidden in shadow. And her chin came up. A combination of excitement, fear and challenge thudded through her veins.

This was it, then. This was the battle she had been waiting all day to engage. She would make him see that his harsh, cutting words had no control over her, and neither was she intimidated. Deep down in her shoes she might be afraid of this man, but she would not show it, and she knew he was powerless against the force of her will.

His question hung in the air, demanding an answer.

She searched in the shadows for his eyes, but she could not see them clearly. Holding her voice steady, with just the right touch of unconcern, she said with dignity, "That is none of *your* business."

He did not move, yet somehow his compellingly masculine stance became more menacing.

"Of course it is, Lindsey. I forced your hand, and you did something completely out of character by going to him and asking for money." His calm delivery belied the powerful emotions he was holding in check.

"How do you know what is in and out of my character?" she asked frostily.

He walked back to the sofa and sat down, his face bleak. "I'm learning," he taunted lowly. "Tell me again what the terms of your loan are with Connor. What did you promise him?" He leaned forward threateningly, his gaze raking her face as she jerked back, stung.

"I promised him nothing," she whispered, even as she flushed at the lie. "Robert is a friend, nothing more."

He seemed to relax slightly. "I think that is Lindsey Wiltse's point of view only." He laughed harshly. "I'm sure Robert Connor would like to be more than just a friend."

"Is it so hard to imagine?" she countered.

He paused, letting his dark eyes sweep her from head to toe. "No, Lindsey, it is not hard to imagine at all." Then his voice hardened. "Tell me one more time that he made no conditions on the loan."

She turned her head away, her face flaming. "All right. There was one condition. One small thing. He wanted the right to continue seeing me, that's all. Nothing else." She faced him proudly. "It was a small enough thing, under the circumstances."

"To continue seeing you," he repeated slowly. "Had you broken with him, then?"

"Yes. No. Sort of. Oh..." She stood up in agitation. "What's the use of all this cat and mouse? You tried to force me to take your father's money, and I won't take it. That's all. I did what I judged to be the best thing under the circumstances. Finished. End of discussion. Just let me write you another check and you can be on your way."

She rose, intending to locate her purse in her bedroom. But Jeremy moved quickly to stand beside her. With an impatient hand he put pressure on her shoulder so that she sank back into the chair. She glared at him while he pulled up the coffee table so that he could sit on it, his knee only a fraction of an inch from her own. Once again he leaned forward.

"You will give Robert Connor his money back," he ordered softly.

Gritting her teeth, she said nothing.

"Lindsey," he reached out to grasp her chin, forcing her around so that she had to look at him. "You never wanted to ask Connor for help. Give it back."

"I won't take money from your father," she spat out.

"Why? You told me that you don't hate him anymore, but I am finding it hard to credit you with speaking the truth."

She jerked her head out of his hold and scrunched back in her chair as far as she could. "Just because I'm trying not to hate him doesn't mean I want to take money from him." She looked away, then turned her gaze back at him. "Why won't you go away? Are you a glutton for punishment, or something?"

"Lindsey, listen to me," Jeremy said in that calm, emotionless tone he used to mask whatever he was feeling. "Let *me* help you. I have plenty of money that has nothing to do with my father. It's true that what I spent so far was out of his account, but I can easily repay him. And I'll arrange for a monthly sum to come directly to you, say about three thousand. Give the loan back to Connor, Lindsey."

She looked at him, disbelieving. "And what would you get out of it? What return would you demand?" she challenged, her face gone unbelievably white. "I am not in the market for a sugar daddy."

"Better me than Robert Connor."

Her hand flew out, to be caught in his grip before it could connect.

"Stop it, Lindsey," he said, instantly remorseful. "I'm sorry. I shouldn't have said it. Put your hand down. Easy now."

She faced him, her eyes wild with her hurt and anger.

"Stop it, I said," he repeated quietly. "Stop thinking the worst of everybody. Stop thinking the worst of me. I'll loan you the money. Interest-free. String-free."

Her skepticism was open. "No strings at all?"

It was his turn to flush, the angry red crawling up his cheeks. "Except one."

She waited questioningly.

"You quit your evening job."

"What?" she asked blankly.

"You quit that po-dunk job at the doughnut shop. You quit it tomorrow. Or preferably, tonight."

"Why?"

"Because I do feel a sense of responsibility, damn it. Even if I personally had nothing to do with the state you're in, my family, my father, has hurt you, has altered your life. Besides, I find myself quite liking you, admiring you. I don't know too many women who would not have given in, bowed under the pressures you're facing every day."

She shook her head fuzzily. "You missed my meaning. Why quit the doughnut shop?"

For an instant he looked startled, as if he realized he had given more away than was required. "You are stretching yourself for nothing at that job," he explained smoothly. "You will break if you continue at your present pace. No one should be doing what you are doing, and you're only being paid pennies, for heaven's sake."

Lindsey's brain was reeling. Maybe he was telling the truth. It would be wonderful to give the money back to Robert Connor. She had not felt comfortable taking it from him, and despite her brave words to Jeremy, she knew Robert would eventually ask for something from her. And there was something else...something she had not shared with either Robert or Jeremy. Corrinne Wiltse, Bradley's mother, had again been pressuring her to give up the children. Maybe if she could prove her solvency, Corrinne would leave her alone. She sighed deeply.

"Lindsey?" Jeremy's voice questioned. "What are you thinking about?"

She turned her head so that she could read what was in his eyes. "You want me to accept the money you have spent on me as a personal loan, and in return you want nothing more than for me to quit my second job?"

He rose and strode across the room to her bookcase, turned, and said a little too nonchalantly, "That's right."

"Would you be willing to write it up legally?" she asked.

He didn't immediately respond, and she knew he was thinking through her reasons for making such a request. "Sure," he said at last, "if that is what you want."

"Good." She took a deep breath. "It would be strictly business, then. And there will be no more talk of a monthly allotment."

He turned abruptly and covered the space between them quickly to once again sit in front of her. He took her suddenly cold hand in his.

"Lindsey, listen to reason," he said grimly. "What I did for you was nothing more than a stopgap measure." He gripped her hand more tightly as she shook her head unreasoningly. "You cannot keep going like this. So I've helped you a little...all right, then, given you a loan. How are you going to pay me back? What happens next month, and the month after that? You are not earning enough to support yourself and your children. And if nothing else matters to you, how are you going to finance the operation Christopher needs?"

She flashed him an accusing look.

"I know. Stop..." He held up his free hand to press his fingers against her open mouth. "Don't say it. Don't say anything. I know what you're thinking anyway: You're thinking that I'm arrogant, that I had no right to invade your privacy. And probably it's all true, but it won't be made any more so by your repeating the obvious. So let's cut out the extraneous garbage and get down to facts. How is Christopher going to have that operation, Lindsey?"

She gave up trying to retrieve her hand. "Now that my bills with the hospital and doctor have been paid," she said stiffly, gathering her pride around her like an old and familiar garment, "I will arrange for the operation immediately."

"All right," Jeremy agreed. "Where will the operation be?"

"Ann Arbor has a children's hospital," she answered.

"How about Chicago?" he suggested dryly.

"Chicago?" she asked in bewilderment.

He grasped her other hand and folded them both together between his own. "There is a children's hospital in Chicago. I could rent you a room there, and I would be there to keep an eye on you."

She stood abruptly, tugging free of him to step away. "You are deliberately misunderstanding me," she accused hotly. "I don't want you to look after me. I look after myself and my own. I do not need you, or want you."

She was trembling again, and she knew that he saw it. She didn't know if her reaction was from anger, or from longing. The truth was she was tempted to let this dominating man do exactly as he wanted. She was so tired, both emotionally and physically. He had been wearing her down. But to give in would be the old story repeated once more.

Bradley had told her over and over again: *I'll take care of you, no need for you to worry about a thing.* And he had weakened her, so that Corrinne Wiltse could follow up with her own brand of truth: *You are incapable of looking after yourself, let alone my grandchildren.*

I am capable.

"All right," Jeremy was saying again with forced patience. "Sit down. I did not mean to get you excited. There are other things we need to discuss."

"Other things..." she repeated faintly. "No." She was practically shouting at him now. "Go away, Jeremy. I have agreed to your loan. I'll pay Robert back. Just send me the legal documents. This discussion is over. It is time for you to go home... to Lucille."

He ignored her, and again taking her hand, pulled her back down into her chair. "What about your future? What about six months from now, Lindsey? What are you going to do to prevent yourself from getting into a financial mess again?"

"Sam has offered me a promotion." She seemed to be answering him in spite of herself.

"What kind of promotion?" his voice sliced through her resentment.

She did not look at him. "As a salesperson. My income will double," she whispered.

"So?" Jeremy queried. "That's good, isn't it? Why can't you look me in the face when you tell me about it? Are you lying, Lindsey?"

Still she would not look at him, and in a sudden movement of exasperation he reached out and jerked her face around. She could not hide from him then the tears she was trying to keep from tumbling down her cheeks, or the pain she did not want him to see.

"What's wrong, now, Lindsey?" he demanded. "Was it a lie?"

"No," she spat at him. "There is a promotion, an opening in the sales force. Sam offered it to me just last week. He said he thought I would be terrific. And it would be a chance to travel..." Her voice faded.

"Travel." He repeated slowly. "How much travel, Lindsey?"

"Sometimes just overnight, other times...a week, maybe two."

She went into his arms then, and he folded her to him tenderly. She felt as if the wall she had built around her heart was breaking. She could feel it cracking, could hear the splintering sound it made inside her breast. *Please, don't be kind,* she pleaded silently. *Don't make me need you. Don't make me dependent. It would be such a great cruelty to make me dependent.*

But he did not hear her silent agonized request.

"What about Christopher and Catherine? Who will watch them while you are away?"

In a fierce sudden movement she twisted out of his arms and strode across the room to the front door. She jerked it open and turned to him, her face white and her eyes anguished. In a ragged voice she said, "It's time for you to go, Jeremy Boulanger. I do thank you for your help, I think. But the rest I must do on my own. You can leave with a clear conscience. Your business here is surely complete. I'm sure there are other things...and people...to interest you in Chicago."

"I'm not leaving, Lindsey," he said, and rose to walk in the direction of her kitchen.

She slammed the door shut. "What are you doing?" she called furiously.

"Making coffee," came his infuriatingly calm reply.

At that she opened her hall closet and pulled out her winter coverings. She had her coat and boots on before Jeremy returned to stand in the kitchen doorway. The clear blue of his eyes were two brilliant sparks of color as he looked down at her blazing eyes. "Where do you think you're going?" he demanded.

"Out," she exploded. "For a walk. Away from you." She pointed her index finger at him in a stabbing motion. "You stay and watch the children." Without thinking of the incongruity of that, she let herself out of her house and began walking blindly down her street.

My house, she muttered to herself. My kitchen, my coffee, my street, my children. Not his. Who did he think he was, anyway? She slammed her feet into the soft snow that lay on the sidewalks around her, noticing it for the first time. Snow was falling even now, she noted. She raised her face to it, feeling its softness on her cheeks and eyelids, letting it wash away her anger and pain. March snow, she thought distractedly, a whispering remnant of the season just passed. These cool, moist droplets did not have the bite of true winter. They were tender, easily melting, holding out the promise of spring. Everyone said this was the coldest winter of the last decade, but you could not tell it by this snow. This snow was gentle, caring, like the touch of Jeremy's hands.

Why was she thinking of Jeremy's hands? It was not his hands that need concern her now. She must think what to do. She must come up with a plan so convincing that it would cause Jeremy to leave her alone. She reached a corner, turned west, and continued walking unseeingly.

Safe. That's what she felt like when Jeremy held her. It had been so long since she felt truly safe. Like the streets of Traverse City. She could walk the streets of Traverse City at night in a soft snowfall in the middle of March and not feel afraid. Not like the streets of Philadelphia, where she had walked so very many years ago.

She had felt safe when Bradley had married her. She had been so overwhelmingly grateful that he had wanted her when she had not even wanted herself. It was only later that she had realized that she had filled an important need for him, too. She was his adoring audience, his undying fan, his loyal servant. And so he had done everything in his power to keep her young. He had carefully taught her about herself: about how she was pretty, and adorable and incapable of taking care of herself.

But she was capable, she told herself. She had coped since Bradley's death. She had done it. But that other voice was also there, whispering viciously. She had done it, but not well. Nobody thought she had done it well. Not Robert Connor, not Corrinne Wiltse, not Jeremy Boulanger. Every one of them was trying to manipulate her so that each could have what he wanted.

The feeling of safety that Jeremy gave her was an illusion. She had already experienced one dominant male in her life; she did not need another. Bradley had made her feel safe, and then had taken away every bit of independence she had ever had. When he had died, she had been completely lost.

She remembered asking Brad to teach her to drive. "No need," Bradley had told her. "I'll take you anywhere you want to go." *Like a child,* she now whispered furiously to herself. She was twenty-seven years old, had two children, had been married. She was not a child. She could cope with things. She was capable.

All right, she answered herself. So she could cope. So she was a grown-up playing in the grown-up leagues. *So tell me, Miss Maturity, how would an adult handle the situation you're in right now?*

Consider the options. Take in all the variables. Make a decision. Stick with it. The thoughts formed a marching rhythm as she walked down the street.

Consider the options. Take in all the variables. Make a decision. Stick with it.

She walked down Front Street and looked unseeing into the windows of the specialty shops there. The snow became deeper. The air grew a little colder. The traffic lights flashed red and yellow.

She thought her options through carefully: One by one she rejected them all, except for what Jeremy Boulanger could offer.

So she would use Jeremy.

Jeremy, however, was himself a variable. He might not like what she had in mind. He might want something in exchange. She might begin to feel more for him than she should. All of these challenges paled beside her desperate need.

Taking a deep breath, she turned to go back to her house, and was shocked at how far she had come. She was at least five miles from her home, and now she would have to walk the long distance back. For the first time she noticed how cold she was. In fact, she was thoroughly chilled, and the waterproofing on her boots had failed her. She could feel icy moisture between her toes. Giving a mental shrug, she started home. Her decision was made—she would deal with Jeremy Boulanger. On her terms.

She walked and planned and thought and planned some more. She was going to take control of her life. She was going to achieve something worthwhile. She would borrow enough money from Jeremy Boulanger to finance her entire college education. He had refused to leave her alone, had practically forced her to accept his help. So she would. She would accept, and more. And when she was done, no man could ever make her dependent again.

She increased her pace, swallowing hard against a rapidly swelling soreness that choked her throat. It did not help that the snowfall had turned fierce, that the earlier softness of the snow had been a mere prelude to a true winter storm. She felt personally betrayed—even the snow had lied to her. Walking became an effort.

When at last she reached her home, every step had become a massive undertaking. Each breath she drew caused a painful rubbing in her throat, and her eyes and nose were watering miserably.

She opened her door, exhausted, only to find Jeremy standing in her living room, glaring at her in the dim light of one lamp, looking like a dark, avenging angel. With a low growl he stepped forward and half-dragged, half-carried her the rest of the way into her house. He kicked the door shut and dropped her onto the sofa.

"Now," he said, his voice a thin cord of taut anger. "Tell me what you think you were doing out there."

Lindsey felt strange, hot and cold at the same time. She could not seem to stop shivering, and it was difficult to hear what Jeremy was saying over the pounding of her heart. Forcing herself upright with great effort, she fixed her eyes on Jeremy. Her chin jutted out. "I was walking," she said slowly, with dignity. She felt proud of herself for being so succinct.

Jeremy muttered something that sounded suspiciously like a curse.

"And you don't have to swear, either," Lindsey said righteously. She was finding it more and more difficult to meet his eyes—she kept seeing two of him. She remembered...she had to implement her decision, the one she had made while she was out walking. She couldn't recall the details right now, but she knew she was going to make an agreement with Jeremy. That was it. But in order to accomplish what she wanted, she would need to be in control. She seemed to have slid down in her seat. She pulled herself upright.

"Do you know what time it is?" Jeremy demanded harshly.

She blinked at him. What time it was? Didn't he have his watch?

"Where have you been?" Jeremy continued to shoot questions at her. "Who were you with?"

"I was walking." Her voice came out in a hoarse croak. "By myself." She waved her arm and pointed an unsteady finger at his chest. "You did not need to worry. I am quite capable of taking care of myself." There, she had that right. She was glad she had remembered. That was very important. "Very important," she told him politely.

"Are you drunk?" Jeremy narrowed his eyes suspiciously.

"No." She straightened again, outraged. Somehow she kept falling over. Sliding down. Or something. "What time did you say it was?"

Jeremy's expression had changed from anger to intense concern. Rising from where he had been sitting in the overstuffed chair, he came to Lindsey and put his hand on her head. "Good heavens," he said, and swept her up in his arms.

"What do you think you're doing?" she sputtered indignantly. "Put me down. I have some things to say to you."

"And I have some things to say to you, Lindsey Wiltse. Tomorrow."

"Tomorrow?" she queried, confused. "You can't stay in my house another night. It's time for you to go Jeremy, back to Chicago. But I need to talk with you first."

She was in her bed, and Jeremy was stripping her clothes off.

"What do you think you're doing?"

"You're burning up with fever, Lindsey. You're really sick."

"But I feel so cold." She shivered.

Then he said something truly unusual: "My dear." And his voice was remarkably husky. He put his arms around her and pulled her onto his lap.

She was wearing nothing but her jeans and bra, but she didn't care. She nuzzled his shoulder, grateful for the warmth of his arms, for his gentle embrace. "I do need to talk with you, Jeremy."

"Tomorrow," he said, his head in her hair.

"Don't be kind, Jeremy."

"Of course not, Lindsey. I'm your enemy, so I can't be kind, right? Now, where are your aspirin?"

"Bathroom . . . bathroom cupboard."

Jeremy laid her down and covered her with her blankets. She lay there shivering and sweating, and wondering why he had pulled away from her. He had felt so good. Too good, but she would think about that tomorrow, also. She snuggled down into the blankets, and wished she had the energy to take her jeans off. She wished Jeremy was still holding her, but when he suddenly reappeared, she was perversely irritated. Especially when he made her sit up and drink some water and take two aspirin tablets.

"You really shouldn't be here," she protested.

"Just take the aspirin, Lindsey."

All he seemed to be doing was giving orders, and she felt she must tell him what she thought of that. She struggled to do so when he put the glass of water on her dresser and then sat down and began to take off his shoes. "What..." Surely that rasping sound wasn't her voice. "What are you . . ."

"Hush," he said, unbuttoning his shirt.

"You can't . . ." she tried again.

"I agree," Jeremy was saying calmly, his voice brisk and businesslike. "I can't stand that short lumpy piece of furniture that's your excuse for a guest bed one more night."

He was going to sleep in her bed. With her in it. She began to thrash wildly, attempting to climb out of bed, only to succeed in tangling herself in the sheets. She looked at him with wide, frightened eyes. His voice became soft; his hands reached out to gentle her.

"Lindsey, relax," he said, as he lay on one side of the bed, stripped to his shorts. "This is not seduction. It is two-thirty in the morning. You are ill. I am tired. We will talk when we wake up. In the meantime I am going to lie here and stretch out. And, now incidentally, I will know whether you are chilled or continue to be feverish. Nothing else, Lindsey. You are safe with me."

Safe. It was a lie. She knew what safe meant. It meant to look out for yourself. She thought she had been safe with her father, but he had abandoned her. She thought she had been safe with Bradley, but he had left her. Jeremy could take his safe and shove it.

She was so tired, too tired to think any further. She relaxed enough to let him straighten the blankets, and lay numbly as he shifted until he found a comfortable spot. She was so cold, she couldn't stop shivering. But to warm herself against him was unthinkable.

She turned on her side with her back to Jeremy's now supine form and closed her eyes. She was asleep almost immediately.

Chapter Seven

This time when she awoke, Lindsey had a feeling of complete disorientation. She groggily turned her head, only to experience a vague, disconnected sense of déjà vu as she noticed the sun shining through her bedroom window. "Oh, no," she muttered. "Not again." She turned to look at her clock and found it missing.

What was today anyway? Monday! She had to go to work! Whatever would Sam be thinking of her unexplained absence? She tried to swing her legs out of bed, only to fall back weakly onto her pillow. What was wrong with her? Groaning, she began to remember, and for a moment she lay listlessly, unwilling to sort things out in her mind.

One fact stood out more clearly than any other: Jeremy Boulanger was still here. Her frustration at his presence had driven her out in a snowstorm. Slowly the events of the preceding night pricked her consciousness.

She realized now she had been ill, too ill to make any coherent sense when she had tried to talk to Jeremy. Still, he had not needed to be so bossy. Another more compelling memory pricked her. With a sudden turn of her head, Lindsey checked the state of her bed, and knew she had not slept alone.

Moaning slightly, Lindsey forced her aching body to a sitting position. Miserably she noticed that her blue jeans and bra had been replaced by a modest white nightgown, and her face flamed at the thought of Jeremy handling her so intimately. She was stumbling to her closet to find her robe when the bedroom door opened and Jeremy strode in. His midnight-blue eyes took in her shaking form, and without a word he moved quickly to her side. She looked at him resentfully before turning her back on him. "Will you please leave while I get dressed?" she asked in a weak, scratchy voice.

He stood for a moment, just watching her from beneath his hooded eyes. His arms hung loosely at his sides, but she sensed a tension that was at odds with his casual stance. She was just about to repeat her command when her bedside telephone rang. Without taking his eyes off Lindsey, Jeremy moved to pick up the phone.

"Hello," he barked into the receiver. Furious that he would take it upon himself to answer her call, Lindsey glared at him.

"What?" Jeremy asked into the phone. "Yes, this is Mrs. Wiltse's house. Who? Ah, yes, she's here. Whom shall I say is calling?" An unholy look of glee passed over Jeremy's features. "Robert Connor...Lindsey has mentioned you to me." Jeremy held out a restraining hand against Lindsey's shoulders as she moved to wrest the phone from him. "In fact, I've been meaning to speak with you for some time about the money she borrowed from you. We would like to pay you back."

We? Where did he get *we*? Again she tried to get the phone from him. Jeremy moved backward, away from her, stopping only when the back of his legs reached her bed.

"Who am I?...Jeremy Boulanger. I'm taking care of Lindsey from now on."

With a low animal growl Lindsey lunged at Jeremy. He neatly sidestepped her, and she found herself sprawled across her bed in a most humiliating fashion. "What was that noise? Oh, that was just Lindsey, tripping over her own bed."

Impotently she pounded her mattress with one balled fist. "Jeremy Boulanger..." she began loudly, only to come to a horrified stop as he continued.

"What? I'm sorry, there's just a little extra noise in here. I'm finding it a bit difficult to hear." Jeremy's voice became low and possessive. "Yes, I know all about your little arrangement, and I want you to know that from this time forward you are to leave Lindsey alone, absolutely. She is in my care." This last phrase was said with slow, deliberate emphasis, before Jeremy slammed the phone onto its holder.

A smug, self-satisfied expression covered Jeremy's face, before he turned grim once more. "You know, you really are a baby, Lindsey. Your Robert Connor didn't sound like a man who expected nothing in return for his loan. In fact, he sounded distinctly disappointed." His voice was heavy with accusation. "Don't you have any sense at all? Even you can't be that innocent. You keep telling me that you can take care of yourself, but I sure don't see any sign of it." Carelessly, he threw himself on the bed beside her, cradling her face between his hands.

She tried to turn her head away from him but could not. She closed her eyes against the tears that were welling there. She had surely cried more since meeting Jeremy than she had during the whole three years since Bradley had died.

Slowly the anger and accusation left his eyes to be replaced by something far more menacing to her peace of mind. Purposefully he lowered his mouth to hers.

Lindsey knew she was drowning. Where she had expected anger and roughness, there was only gentleness and tender-

ness. It went on forever, and sometime during that kiss
things changed between them, so that she found herself
kissing him back. She knew she had been waiting for this
moment since that time in her car. So this is what a kiss
really felt like, she thought, this sharing between two people. Bradley, why didn't you let me know?

When Jeremy at last pulled away, she looked at him,
dazed, and only then realized that his hand had crept inside
her loosened robe. "Lindsey?" His voice formed the question tenderly.

She looked at him blankly. "What?" Then she realized
what he was asking. "No," she said in a voice that sounded
strangely foreign. "No, of course not."

She tried to roll away from him. At her movement he
lifted his own body, and she rose from the bed, feeling hot
and flushed. "I can't think what . . ." she began. "That is,
really, I'm sorry. I've led you on . . . I guess. That's unforgivable in a man's eyes, isn't it?" She turned away from
where he was sitting on her bed. "I'm truly sorry, but I
can't . . . That is, I won't let you . . ."

A slow smile seemed to be beginning at the corner of Jeremy's mouth. "It's all right, Lindsey. I took you by surprise. Not that it wouldn't be wonderful, but I think you're
probably right, it's too soon, and you're still ill."

Of course it was too soon. It would always be too soon.
She would never, ever, have an affair with Jeremy Boulanger. She began to button up her robe, finding the simple task
incredibly difficult.

"Oh, for heaven's sake." Jeremy's voice had lost all trace
of softness. "Go back to bed, Lindsey. You're hardly well
enough to walk across your own bedroom floor."

She turned to face him. "I can't," she replied, breathing
hard. "I have to take a shower. I have to go to work. Sam
will be wondering why I haven't called." He was watching
her from a face that had gone strangely still. "And where is
my clock? What time is it?"

Jeremy made a show of looking at the slim gold watch on his wrist. "It's past three o'clock, Lindsey."

"Three o'clock?" she exclaimed. "I've missed a whole day's work?" Even to herself she sounded slightly hysterical. "What will Sam Arnold think of me?"

"He knows, Lindsey. I called him for you."

That took a moment to sink in. She raised wide eyes to his. "And my children?"

"Catherine is in school. Christopher is here. He's napping at the moment."

She was having trouble standing up straight. She reached out to put a hand onto her dresser, but it was lower than she thought and she stumbled. Again she felt Jeremy's arms go around her. "Lindsey, today is Tuesday," he said carefully.

"Tuesday? But that is...impossible. Last night was Sunday..."

"You made yourself sick walking in the snow. You've been burning with fever."

She sagged against him. "Who...who took care of me?"

Gently he lowered her again to her bed. "Three guesses."

She struggled to accept what he was telling her. "Why are you doing this?" she asked at last. "Why are you being so kind?"

"Why not?"

"And you've slept in my bed for two nights?"

He grinned, that full-fledged, totally wicked grin that, dazed as she was, still took her breath away. "If that's a thank you, you're welcome. I told you Sunday night, I'm through with that misguided excuse of a guest bed."

Her eyes rounded owlishly. "But the children—"

"The children are lucky to have me here. You are lucky to have me here. Besides, I may have shared your bed, but nothing happened. More's the pity."

She began to form another objection in her mind, but he was ahead of her. "That is enough for now on the subject.

You're not up to a real argument—yet. Take your medicine instead."

She eyed the spoonful of gummy liquid distastefully. "What is it?"

"Antibiotics. Dr. Montgomery prescribed it. He said you have pneumonia coupled with extreme exhaustion and malnutrition."

"I don't remember going to see the doctor."

"You didn't." Jeremy's voice was grim. "He came here."

"Now I know you're lying. Doctors don't make house calls. You go to the emergency room."

"All right. Don't believe me. Just take your medicine."

Meekly, she did.

The next time she woke she actually felt quite a bit better. The curtains were pulled, and the room was dark. She was lying on her side, and her eyes automatically sought her clock, only to discover—again—that it wasn't there.

She reached out to turn on her beside lamp, but the sound of someone breathing deeply pulled her up short. He was fast asleep, right next to her in her own bed. She pulled her arm carefully back to rest on the blankets, resisting an urge to reach out and touch him. He had obviously felt no such compunction; one of his legs was covering both of hers, and his hand was curved around her breast. Her heart caught in her throat. Forcing herself to breathe evenly, she lay very still and tried to think.

What was Jeremy doing to her? He had shown a different side of himself these past few days. It was hard to remember that she had once thought him cold and unfeeling. Right now, with him curved around her, she was not cold or unfeeling either.

It felt good, having him there. She remembered his kiss, and her heart seemed to stop. Then, just for a moment, she allowed her hand to reach up and touch his. It was only a soft touch, and she decided immediately to remove it. But when she tried to put her hand in a safe place on her pillow, his larger one snaked out and grabbed it, pulling her even closer. She froze, conscious of her very vulnerable position should he truly waken.

Lindsey had slept so much in the past few days that sleep was now impossible. She lay there, miserable, her eyes peering into the darkness around her. She heard him breathe, felt the length of his hard male body against her own, smelled his faint manly odor. It seemed a slow eternity had passed before the sound of an alarm surprised her. She had assumed her clock was not anywhere near, but its insistent demand from under the bed was very real. "Umm," Jeremy said, and reached down to the floor on his side of the bed to turn the alarm off.

"Jeremy?" she asked softly.

"You're awake." Relief was evident in his tone.

"What time is it?" She tried to sound normal, as if waking in his arms were an everyday occurrence.

"It's ten minutes before I have to get up in order to get Catherine off to school."

So he liked a slow wake-up in the morning. She decided to remember that, one more piece of information that she knew about Jeremy Boulanger, then wondered why she bothered.

"You may like to lie abed in the mornings, but I have things to do. I'm feeling ever so much better," she said lightly, and, just as lightly, tried to remove his hand from where it lay atop of hers on her breast. His hold on her tightened. "What do you have to do?" he asked huskily.

Oh dear. Oh dear. She could not think of a single thing. Jeremy shifted his body slightly so that she was pulled against him, and she realized hopelessly that he was not wearing any clothes at all. His hand began a slow massage up and down her arm, over her breast, down to the flat of her stomach, and then made the same trip all over again.

"What do you think you're doing?" She tried to sound indignant, but she was afraid she sounded merely breathless.

"Holding you," he answered against her temple, and then he moved his head so that his lips were touching her neck. He lifted her hair away so that his mouth could have freer access to the skin there, then his hand, again, resumed that slow exploration over the front of her body.

It felt so good. Just touching and being touched felt so good. She would have to stop it, of course, but in the meantime maybe she could enjoy this wonderful feeling for just a few more minutes. Jeremy had raised himself up, and his lips were tracing a pattern of liquid fire down her bare arm. She shivered. He turned her onto her back, and his lips found hers in a kiss of exquisite exploration. She accepted his mouth hungrily, greedily. His hand moved down to her thigh, and he began to pull her nightgown up, his lips never leaving hers. Warning bells shrilled like a thousand telephones inside her head.

Telephones. Telephone. The telephone was ringing. The realization jolted her, and she tried to shove Jeremy away.

"Let it ring," he ordered, his voice deep with desire.

"No." She cleared her throat, feeling alive and sensuous and frightened. "Nobody ever calls me this early in the morning, Jeremy. I'd better see who it is."

"All right," he said, and rolled off her enough to allow her to raise herself on her elbow.

She fumbled for the bedside receiver. "Hello?" Jeremy's right hand had renewed its seductive movement over her body.

"Lindsey?" Corrinne's smooth voice swept over her like an icy shower. Lindsey tightened her hand over the mouthpiece and shifted into a sitting position. "Lindsey, is that you?" Corrinne repeated impatiently.

"What do you want, Corrinne?" Lindsey asked frigidly. Jeremy's hand had stilled on her hip.

"Lindsey, my dear, have you given any more thought to my proposition?"

What an ugly word, with so many meanings. Proposition. Just what Jeremy was doing, also. He had been trying to make love to her and had nearly succeeded, but it meant nothing to him, she was sure. He probably thought he deserved a physical reward for taking care of her. Well, she had not asked him to stick around. She would never have been sick if he had just left her alone. It was his presence that had driven her out into the snowstorm. He had a lot to answer for.

"Lindsey?" Corrinne's cultivated, patrician voice focused her attention back on her mother-in-law.

"Why are you calling me this early?" she asked sharply.

"Is this too early?" Corrinne asked. "I was sure you would be up, getting Catherine ready for school. She isn't sick, is she?"

"No."

Corrinne's voice was honeyed acid. "Perhaps you're simply having a hard time getting out of bed. Because you're not alone, are you, Lindsey?"

Lindsey sucked in her breath. She almost blurted out the incriminating truth before her passion-fogged mind recognized the trap Corrinne had laid for her. "Of course I'm alone," she snapped.

"Lindsey, dear, you make a very bad liar. I know all about him. I've had you followed by a private detective. It cost me the earth over these past few months, but these last few days have made it all worthwhile. So it's no use denying to me that you've taken a lover. I have his picture here in my hand, and he's really quite handsome. Tall. Darkhaired. Expensive clothing. Expensive car. I must congratulate you on attracting him."

Lindsey closed her eyes. She could almost hear Corrinne purring spitefully.

"The court is going to love this, Lindsey. Not only are you incapable of providing for the children financially, your morals leave a great deal to be desired. I've got quite a long list of ways in which you're falling short as a mother. I think you'd better agree to my proposition. A hundred thousand dollars is a lot of money, Lindsey."

"No!" Lindsey shouted into the phone before slamming it down.

Jeremy reached out to cover her hand with his own. "What was that about?" he asked, no passion in his voice now.

She turned on him savagely. "About you, Jeremy Boulanger," she said, tears running down her cheeks. "Why did you have to come here? Why couldn't your father and you have left me alone? You've ruined everything."

"Now wait just a minute," Jeremy growled. "Who was that?"

"None of your business," Lindsey hissed at him, and rolled off the bed. "None of your damned business." She pulled on her robe and began to pace feverishly. She turned to him and began to talk violently. "Good times are over, Jeremy. Time for you to get up. Time for you to get going. Time for you to listen to me, for a change."

Jeremy turned and sat up in the bed. "Who was it, Lindsey? Who is Corrinne?"

"Nobody in particular. Nobody important. Just the children's grandmother, their wealthy grandmother. Corrinne Wiltse, of the Philadelphia Wiltses. She would make such a better parent for the children than I. After all, she has so much money. And I am so p-o-o-r." Lindsey spelled it out for him. "Incapable, poor, and now, immoral."

She turned on him like an angry, spitting cat. "Immoral, and guess who with? One Jeremy Boulanger, who has spent three nights in my house with me and my children. She has a detective's report on you, Jeremy. They even have your picture. So while you were busy seducing me this morning,

Corrinne with her dirty little mind and her great big bank account has got it all added up.'' She glowered at him viciously. ''You've really done it now, did you know that? You with your kindness and your desire to help poor widow Wiltse, when I told you and told you I didn't want your help.''

She grabbed her hairbrush and jabbed it at him. ''So how do you help me out of this one, huh? Well, I'll tell you how to help. Get the hell out of here. Get out of my bed, out of my house, out of my life!''

Jeremy watched the waving hairbrush warily. ''How will my leaving help, now, Lindsey? The damage is already done.''

She closed her eyes in an effort at control. ''It...will...help...*me!*'' she shouted at him furiously.

He grabbed the hairbrush out of her hand and put it carefully on her dresser. ''I've got a better idea,'' he said mildly.

''Jeremy—''

''Tell her we're engaged.''

That stopped her. Her mouth fell open. Her breasts heaved. Her eyes dilated.

''Now I know you're crazy,'' she finally managed, before she turned on her heel to go and wake her children.

Jeremy didn't leave. He insisted on helping the children get ready for their day—first Catherine for school, then Christopher for the sitter's. ''We could keep him here with us,'' he told Lindsey, ''but I think we need time to talk, don't you?''

''No,'' she said. ''We do not need to talk. We do not need to do anything. You need to get out of here, before you do any more damage.'' She banged her clenched fist on the kitchen table. ''I don't want you around anymore. What happened between us this morning was a complete aberration. I don't even like you.''

Blue-black anger flared deep within his eyes. "You talk too much," he said.

Then he drove Christopher to the sitter's. Before leaving, Jeremy turned to Lindsey. "Stay here," he ordered. "Don't think of going anywhere. I told your boss you would be out at least a week, so there's absolutely no need for you to go to work. You're recuperating from a very nasty illness, so just don't think of going anywhere."

She tossed her head angrily, but she stayed. He was, after all, right. She felt incredibly weak. What was it he had said...pneumonia coupled with malnutrition? She really would have to force herself to eat more. And somehow Jeremy had convinced her doctor to make a house call. The hard grim line of her mouth softened as she realized that Jeremy had cared enough to stay with her when no one else had been available.

She began to feel a little ashamed of her outburst this morning. After all, Jeremy knew nothing about her mother-in-law, with her threats and constant attempts to have the children put in her care. But that Corrinne had called when she was just about to let Jeremy make love to her...

"No excuse," she muttered. "It was no excuse to fly off the handle like that."

When Jeremy returned an hour later, he brought with him three sacks full of groceries and a grim face. Without even greeting Lindsey, who was sitting bundled in a blanket on the living room sofa, he went directly to the kitchen and put things away, just as if he had every right to do so, as if he lived there. When he had finished, Lindsey heard him fill the drip coffee-maker, and then he brought her her medicine, his face absolutely expressionless. "Take this," he said, and thrust the pharmaceutical bottle at her, along with a spoon. He placed a glass of orange juice on the table next to her.

"All right," she said meekly. "Thank you, Jeremy." Only the slight lifting of an eyebrow responded to her conciliatory tone. He went back to the kitchen and she could tell from the sounds he was making that he had sat down at her table with the morning paper. She was being purposefully ignored.

All right, she told herself. Now or never.

"Jeremy," she called, but her voice came out in a cracked rattle. She cleared her throat and tried again. "Jeremy?"

She thought for a minute that he wasn't going to answer her, even though she heard him put the paper down. When he did, his voice was tight, controlled, angry. "Yes?" he said curtly.

"Please come in and sit with me for a minute," she requested.

Again that pause, as if he was debating with himself how he would respond to her. She heard the sound of a chair being scraped across the floor, and he came into the living room. She eyed him warily, sensing that his bland visage was hiding a terrible anger, that he was controlling himself with great effort. He moved with the lean grace of a hungry panther to sit in the easy chair that was across from her sofa. "Yes?" he said at last, distantly.

She straightened. Her chin jutted out. She really hated it when he took that tone with her. After all, she had not asked him to seek her out. What did he expect, that she would immediately fall in gratitude at his feet?

Jeremy's gaze raked over her face, and with a motion of disgust he got up and headed back to the kitchen.

"No," she said. "Wait." He half-turned, his eyes on her face, his mouth in a stern, straight line. His left eyebrow rose.

She took a deep breath. "I'm sorry," she said stiffly. "I didn't mean half of what I said this morning. I'm not sure I meant any of it. I was scared, Jeremy. Corrinne has been threatening to take Christopher and Catherine ever since Bradley died."

Jeremy returned to his seat in the living room. His nostrils flared slightly.

"You're not making this easy," she accused him bitterly.

"Good," he said with exquisite politeness. "Good."

She turned away from him. Her arm had been resting on the sofa end, now she brought up her tightly balled fist so that her chin could rest on it. She was thinking a little more clearly, and she was remembering the decision she had made Sunday night as she had walked in the snow.

"You took me by surprise, you know, that night in the doughnut shop. It wasn't fair," she said, and realized that she sounded like a petulant child. She turned to face him, almost losing her nerve at the burning she saw in his eyes. "Jeremy, I do need help." The words tasted like sandpaper in her mouth.

He sat back and put his feet up on her coffee table, his hands behind his head, and regarded her solemnly. His hair was slightly ruffled, as if he had combed it with his hands while he had been in the kitchen. His sweater stretched across his chest, and she knew from recent memory how well muscled he was there. Again she looked away. "Thank you for taking care of me when I was sick," she said in a small voice. "And for caring for Catherine and Christopher also."

"You're welcome."

"Did you really get Dr. Montgomery to come here to the house?"

"Yes."

She sighed.

"You said you needed help," Jeremy prodded cruelly.

She flushed painfully. "I've thought about it," Lindsey replied indirectly, "and I've reached a decision. I'll take the money you've spent on me so far, as a loan. I'll give Robert his money back. You were right, I really didn't want to take it from him, but at the time it seemed the best solution."

She squared her shoulders. "You've been right about a great many things. Anyway, I have a plan, and this is it—if I could borrow living money for a while, I would like to use it to return to school, to college. I would like to be a teacher.

I like children, and a job like that would interfere as little as possible with the lives of my own children once they were both in school. After I finished college, I could start paying you back, at some acceptable portion every month."

A long silence was her only answer. She shifted uncomfortably. She felt her face go a bright red. "I guess the idea wasn't so—so good, after all," she stammered. "Forget it, then."

She would have risen, but it had taken all of her energy to shower while Jeremy was out. She was aware of an overwhelming sensation of defeat. It had seemed like such a good plan on Sunday night, when she had thought it out. She would love to go to college, had wanted to even during her marriage, but Bradley had never thought it necessary for her to do so. She still wanted to do it, and somehow she would find a way.

She had thought that Jeremy would actually approve of her plan. For once, she had been sure that he would understand her need to be self-sufficient. Now, stealing a look at his implacable face, she realized that she could not have been more wrong. He was just like everyone else.

From somewhere inside her she felt a tight ball of anger and frustration, and her hands clenched tightly. Bradley was wrong. For three years she had proved how wrong he was. Corrinne was wrong. The children were happy, well-behaved and had a strong sense of self-worth. Robert was wrong, and Jeremy, sitting there looking so full of condemnation, was wrong, too. Other women had faced challenges worse than hers and succeeded. She would face this.

She was tired of seeing herself through other people's eyes. She wanted to be defined by herself, for herself. She turned to face Jeremy. "You probably don't believe I can do it, do you?" she asked angrily. "Well, I can. And I thought you wanted to help me, but maybe you define that word differently than I do. You probably define help by meaning that you want me to be dependent on you.

"If I'm dependent, then I'm more likely to agree to whatever you want, no matter what it is. If I'm dependent then you can feed your macho male ego because you were able to help the helpless little Lindsey Wiltse." She stood on shaky feet. "Well, I don't need your kind of help, Mr. Boulanger. I would have managed if you had not come into my life, and I will still manage."

Jeremy had risen, too, and he had such a look of controlled violence about him that in spite of her own great and righteous anger she shivered. "And you can stop looking at me like that," she said. "You don't own me, and you have no right to sit in judgment on me."

The anger in Jeremy's face had been replaced by a carefully shuttered expression, then that, too, seemed to pass to leave something like compassion in his eyes. "Do sit down, Lindsey," he suggested gently, "before you fall down. Dr. Montgomery said you wouldn't be truly well for at least another week. Now, sit down. All this arguing and shouting won't do your body any good at all."

She did sit down, only because she began to feel dizzy, and she was finding it more and more difficult to focus on Jeremy, or anything else, for that matter.

Jeremy crossed over the room to lower his large frame by her side. Gently he put his arms around her and pulled her close, holding her head down onto his chest. She could hear his heart beating, and gave a little sigh. This felt so right, she admitted to herself. She liked being held like this.

She sighed again, confused by all the emotions and thoughts that swirled around inside her. She was still trying to make sense of her own thoughts when Jeremy started speaking again, and she had to ask him to repeat himself.

"I said, my independent Lindsey, that I think your plan has merit. We would probably be able to work out the terms of a loan such as you suggested. Of course, as your lender, I would have certain requirements of my own."

"Oh?" she managed to say quite coolly, and tried halfheartedly to pull away from the comforting embrace of his arms.

He tightened his hold on her. "Oh," he confirmed dryly. "Not the least of which is equal to what you were willing to do with Connor. I want to keep seeing you, Lindsey. Hold still, and let me finish," he ordered softly, as she tried to twist around so that she could see the expression in his eyes.

"Christopher will have to have his operation, you will need to give notice at both your jobs, and you will need to relocate to the Chicago area, where institutions of higher learning are plentiful. In return, I will loan you sufficient money to accomplish your goal of getting a college education, and we can work out the terms of payback at some future date. Is that satisfactory?"

"You're asking a lot," she mumbled into his shirt front.

"Not half of what I'd like to ask," he answered her, stroking her face and arm with a firm touch.

"Stop that," she said.

Immediately his hands stilled, but he did not let her go. "That leaves only Corrinne to be dealt with," he said calmly. "Have you any suggestions for dealing with your mother-in-law?"

"Not right now," Lindsey answered through a haze of pleasurable feeling aroused by his strong embrace. "But I'll think of something a little less extreme than announcing a false engagement."

"Leave her to me, Lindsey Wiltse," Jeremy said. "I'll take care of Corrinne, and whether your little independent soul desires it or not, I'll take care of you."

Jeremy stayed in Lindsey's home for one more week. He pampered Lindsey back to health, and he absolutely won over Christopher and Catherine. Together Lindsey and Jeremy made a tentative timetable for the move to Chicago and her registration at college. He spent time on the telephone making arrangements for Christopher's operation at a major hospital. He insisted she call Sam Arnold and tell him what was going on, so that, he said, she wouldn't be faced with giving her notice when he wasn't there to support her.

During that strange, wonderful week Jeremy made no further demands on her. It seemed that now that things were settled, he lost the compulsion to seduce her into compliance. Still, he did touch her whenever he seemed to want to, and there were times when he would come up to her when she was standing at the stove or the kitchen counter, and wrap his arms around her, moving his lips against her neck and cheek. He made no secret of the fact that he desired Lindsey, but it seemed that he was waiting for a sign from her that her needs equaled his own.

That sign was the one thing she was determined not to give him. It was the hardest thing she had ever done, especially since he refused to budge from her bed. She finally gave up trying to talk him into going back to the living room sofa.

When, in a moment of frustration, she suggested to him that he should find a motel somewhere, he only laughed, and replied mockingly that he could think of no place he would rather be at night than in her bed. So she attempted to sleep on the sofa herself, and Jeremy laughingly carried her back to her bedroom.

"What's the matter, Lindsey?" he had taunted. "Afraid that in the middle of the night you might want me, or something?" Flushing deeply, she had finally admitted defeat.

She secretly enjoyed sleeping in the circle of Jeremy's arms, but not for the world would she admit such a thing to him. She was already so close to being absolutely in love with him that she was sure that any more compromises on her part would push her over that edge just as surely as if she deliberately jumped.

Lindsey would awaken in the middle of the night to feel the sure sign of his desire against her, and an answering response would rush through her own body, and she knew that indeed she did want Jeremy, but was terrified of the wanting. How could she explain to him that Bradley had always made her feel like such a little girl, so that the only lovemaking she had ever known had been on such an unequal level that it had left her feeling insecure and unsure of her own femininity? How could she tell him that she feared he was merely playing with her, that she was a novelty to him, for surely any man as rich and handsome as Jeremy could have his pick of women? How could she explain that with children to raise, she simply did not have the right to give into the whim of a moment?

And most of all, how could she explain that already he would leave a great gaping hole in her life when his interest in her and her children waned, and how much worse it would be for her to bear his leaving if she actually allowed herself to have an affair with him? For, except for that halfhearted reference to being engaged the morning Corrinne had called, he had never spoken of anything permanent, or lasting, or indeed anything more than wanting. And always there was Lucille, that woman he had contacted in Chicago, whom he never mentioned and whom she was afraid to ask about.

So the week passed, brittle in its intensity, until Lindsey was pronounced well by the doctor and Jeremy at last left for Chicago and whatever he did there. With only an informal promise of "I'll be back," and a light kiss on her cheek, he was gone, leaving her bereft and unsettled. Even the children had gotten real, affectionate hugs from him, and he had promised to bring them presents when he returned.

She had stiffened at that, but if Jeremy noticed, he said nothing. He eased himself into his silver Porsche, and with a general wave for the three of them standing in her doorway, he gunned his engine and drove off. It wasn't until hours later that Lindsey discovered Jeremy's travel kit still in her bathroom, and one of his sport coats hanging in her closet.

Chapter Eight

In late April Lindsey moved with her two children to a northern suburb of Chicago. She contacted the doctor that Jeremy had found for Christopher, and a day in July was set for her son's operation. She applied and was accepted by Northwestern University, a process that was easier than she had hoped. She wanted to apply for financial aid, but Jeremy had been adamantly opposed to the idea. When she had protested that such expensive tuition would only add to the amount that she would eventually have to repay him, he had been impossibly angry. He informed her that if he wanted to make a gift of her college education, she had better damned well accept it. She had shouted back that she would pay back every penny, but she had not applied for financial aid.

She had not yet heard from Corrinne, but she knew it was just a matter of time before her mother-in-law would make her move. She documented every financial transaction between Jeremy and herself, in preparation for the day she would have to prove her worth as a mother in the courts.

Lindsey loved the home that Jeremy had found for her. It was much bigger than the little house in Traverse City, and the added space was a luxury. Her new home was a two-story, older brick Georgian, with a full basement, located on a quiet, tree-lined residential street, and the rent was surprisingly affordable. The spacious interior was newly painted, and the carpeting was thick and comfortable.

For the first time in a long while, Lindsey relaxed. Her hair grew thick and glossy again, her complexion began to glow, her eyes grew clear and untroubled. She knew that Jeremy might, at some later date, try to extract a payment from her that had nothing to do with money, but so far he had not come to collect. In fact, after seeing her safely moved and settled, he had not come around very much at all. She allowed herself the bittersweet emotion of hope. Maybe things would turn out all right after all. The decision she had reached on that snowy night in March had been a wise one, she congratulated herself, for her circumstances were vastly improved and her future looked much brighter.

She thought more about Jeremy than she cared to admit. It was, however, difficult to keep him out of her mind when his largess constantly surrounded her. She accepted with resignation his absence from her life—she had not seen him in over a month. She could only conclude that whatever had attracted him to her had paled, now that his responsibility toward her had been taken care of, and she congratulated herself again and again that she had not had even a brief affair with Jeremy Boulanger.

Twice she had seen mention of him in the Chicago papers, accompanying wealthy socialite Lucille Abbott to some high-society function or other. From the pictures, Lucille appeared very sophisticated and very beautiful. Lindsey was sure Lucille and Jeremy moved in circles far removed from her own ordinary life-style. In fact, she doubted Jeremy even thought about her now.

In June the doctor called and said that Christopher's operation had been moved up to the next week. Lindsey remembered that Jeremy had asked her to contact him when she heard definitely when her son's operation was to be scheduled, so reluctantly she called the office number he had left with her. Jeremy's secretary answered with a cool, professional voice, and told her Mr. Boulanger was out of town. She hung up without leaving a message, feeling relieved that she had not had to talk to him, after all.

The day of Christopher's operation arrived quickly. Lindsey had arranged for Catherine to stay at a neighbor's so she would be free to stay at the hospital.

Now, sitting in the sterile hospital waiting room, Lindsey laid her head against the back of her chair and closed her eyes. She had not expected to feel fear, but here she was, stiff and tired from its unexpected presence. While the operation had a good chance of succeeding, if it failed her little Christopher would be more handicapped than ever, and she could not keep the anxiety from swelling within her. She looked at the large institutional clock hanging on the wall, and realized hopelessly that less than an hour had passed of the intricate four-hour surgery.

A familiar, prickly feeling made its way up her spine, and Lindsey straightened in response to it. Her eyes flew open to meet the furious gaze of Jeremy Boulanger, from where he was standing rigidly in the doorway of the waiting room. His eyes flicked over her contemptuously before he strode to where she was sitting. With harsh, jagged movements he drew off his suitcoat and tie before he lowered himself into the chair next to hers. She didn't look at his face again, and she did not speak. His anger barely registered. A warm, happy glow began in her center and spread slowly throughout her body.

"You had to do it yourself, didn't you?" he asked savagely. "I asked you expressly to let me know when anything was going to happen with Christopher, but you couldn't perform the common courtesy of contacting me."

She closed her eyes, trying to ward off his attack, but he continued in a furious voice. "I've left you alone. I haven't rushed you. I think things are going fine between us, and then I get a call from the damn doctor wanting to know why I'm not here to support you when you're obviously terrified."

She breathed in, then out; in, then out. She could feel his anger, but she couldn't seem to make any sense out of what he was saying. Her relief at his unexpected appearance was so intense, it hurt. Slowly, as if it had a will of its own, her hand slid over to his arm. She clutched his arm through his shirtsleeve, her nails digging through the fine fabric to find the reassuring warmth of his skin. His other hand came up to cover hers, and with a sigh she opened her eyes to steal a glance at him. He was sitting very still, his eyes staring ahead inflexibly.

"I did try to call, last week, but your secretary said you were out of town," she said in a low voice.

His gaze turned to encompass her face. "Did you leave a message?"

She shook her head wordlessly.

"Why not?" he asked with cutting politeness. "Damn it, Lindsey, I could wring your lovely neck."

"Why?" She heard her voice shaking slightly. "You've done your duty by us, certainly. I didn't want to burden you unnecessarily."

He swore savagely.

"Okay, Jeremy, you've impressed me by the depth of your vocabulary," she threw at him, aware at last of the strength of his anger.

"And you've impressed me that you don't need me at all," he retorted sardonically, prying her still-tight fingers off his arm. "What's this, Lindsey?" he asked. "The hand of a calm mother handling her concern without the help of anyone?''

For the first time she became aware of the clawlike hold she had forced on Jeremy's arm. She tried to smile, but gave up the effort when tears threatened perilously close. ''I didn't know there was anyone to care,'' she said softly. ''I'm glad you came, Jeremy. I would have made more of an effort to get in touch with you, but I really didn't think you would want to be bothered, that's all. Now that you're here, I'm so glad. Thank you for coming.'' She paused, then continued hesitantly. ''I hope you didn't have to leave anything too important.''

He smiled briefly. ''Nothing too important, Lindsey. Just a board meeting that's been scheduled for two months.''

''Oh.''

''Just don't ever assume I don't want to be bothered again.''

''All right.'' And she did smile at him then, a full, radiant smile that softened his harsh features and brought his arm around her. She felt joyous, full to the brim with happiness. It felt so good to have a friend in this strange city, someone she could depend on. It felt so wonderful just knowing she was no longer alone.

They sat quietly for a moment, her hand locked in his, and she tried to sort out this thing that had just happened between them. She could feel Jeremy begin to relax, and then she felt him begin to massage her hand with his thumb. She remembered the nights when they had slept together, how right that had felt, even though she had denied it since. This felt right, too, sitting with him and drawing comfort in this most frightening moment of her life.

And it was here, in the artificial light of a hospital room, waiting while her son had surgery that would either correct his clubfeet forever or leave him permanently in braces, that she finally admitted what she had tried to deny, that she loved Jeremy Boulanger.

Yet with all the wisdom of her heart, she understood that he would never love her back, not with the same intensity she was feeling. He might desire her for a little while, as he had done in the past. He might enjoy making sure things were all right in her life. But she would be fooling herself if she once, even once, thought that a man like Jeremy Boulanger could love her.

Suddenly Jeremy interrupted her thoughts, asking, "How much longer?"

"Another two hours," she said, avoiding his eyes.

"I think you could use a cup of coffee," he said firmly. "Why don't we go down to the cafeteria and get some. We could leave word at the nurses' desk where we are."

"All right," she acquiesced helplessly, knowing that at this moment of revelation she would follow him anywhere.

All the way down the corridor, into the elevator, past the registration desk, into the hospital cafeteria, Jeremy kept her hand tucked in the crook of his arm. She walked in a cloud at his side, pretending for just a moment that her life was always like this, that they were a couple, in love, married. *Married?*

This would never do. She pulled her hand from his abruptly.

"Is something the matter?" he asked quizzically.

"No."

But when she ended up sitting at a table across from him, she found she could not meet his eyes. It would be too humiliating for him to know her newly realized secret. He knew too many of her secrets already, when she knew hardly anything about him. That was something she could rectify, right now.

"What do you do for a living?" she blurted, when the silence between them began to be uncomfortable.

"I'm an investment broker, Lindsey," he answered, and reached over the table to take one of her hands in his. Her attempt to pull away was quickly thwarted as he tightened his hold.

Didn't he know what he was doing to her? Despairing, she knew the answer to be negative. How could he know when he did not feel the same way? She strove to keep the conversation going. "And you're good at it, I suppose."

He smiled rather crookedly. "Yes, Lindsey, I'm good at it. One of the best, as a matter of fact."

She found she was able to look at him after all. "And you're proud of that success."

He inclined his head. "For a long time the success I achieved was all that was important in my life. Whenever something becomes most important to you, above all else, the chances for success become greater."

"Do you still feel that way?" she asked cautiously.

"Now my life has become more interesting."

She waited for him to continue, and so was surprised when he changed the subject. "And you?" he asked. "How are things going for you?"

"Quite well," she replied with admirable calm. "The children have settled in nicely, and you know I've been accepted as a freshman at Northwestern University." She smiled. "That will feel strange: Me, a mother and a widow, sitting side by side with all those eighteen-year-olds. Actually, the thought quite terrifies me."

His hand let go of hers as he reached for his coffee. "I've got a feeling that you're going to do just fine, Lindsey Wiltse," he said, but he was looking at the table, not at her, and she found herself doubting his sincerity. Again the silence between them lengthened.

"Where's Catherine?" he finally asked.

"At a neighbor's. She makes friends so easily."

"Now that's one quality she didn't get from you," he mocked teasingly.

She winced. Her soul shriveled. He was so right. She did not make friends easily at all. It had been so long since she felt she could actually trust anyone, which was probably why she was feeling so close to Jeremy now. In fact, she thought, all these thoughts of love were more likely misrepresentations of gratitude. Jeremy had proved trustworthy, had showed up here at the hospital when she hadn't believed he really wanted to come. So, like an adolescent, she had mistaken feelings of grateful affection for love. Of course she didn't love him. She felt so relieved that she decided to tell him how she really felt. "I'm friends with you," she said softly, and smiled at him.

His eyes flashed and held hers. She found she was holding her breath. *Oh no, Jeremy,* she thought, *don't say anything. Don't make me hope for anything more, when I've just decided that friendship will do very nicely indeed.* His eyes flickered over her face, and whatever he was going to say died in his throat.

"Well, friend," he said easily. "Tell me what your plans are for this week that Christopher is in the hospital. What are you going to do with Catherine, for instance? Surely she isn't staying the whole week at the neighbor's?"

"No, but I will manage."

Irritation creased his forehead. "Sure, Lindsey Wiltse, you always manage," he said curtly. She let her hands rest on her lap as she carefully studied her napkin.

"Come on," he said, sounding angry, "let's go see how Christopher is doing."

They were back in the waiting room only a few minutes when the doctor strode toward them, smiling broadly. "Ah, Jeremy, I see you made it after all," he said, before turning to Lindsey.

"Although only time will tell for sure, Mrs. Wiltse, it looks like the operation has been a success. I'm very pleased. And that is one brave little boy you have. You know the last thing he said to me before we put him out? He told me to tell you not to worry, that he was going to be all right.

And he is all right,'' he continued, rubbing his hands together. "He's going to be just fine."

Relief washed over Lindsey, leaving her lightheaded. Tears formed in her eyes as, smiling happily, she turned to the doctor and threw her arms around him, planting a swift kiss on his cheek. She whirled, laughing, and flung herself into Jeremy's arms, hugging him and planting a kiss on his cheek, too.

Then, when she would have let go of Jeremy, his arms were still around her, urging her closer, and his lips were on hers, and this wasn't a kiss between friends at all. Jeremy was kissing her passionately, as if he had missed her and had hungered for her and was trying to assuage his need in one, all-encompassing embrace. Surprised, she struggled against him momentarily before melting in his arms. Her hands found their way into the thickness of his hair, while his hands were also busy, one clasping her head to him with a strong grip around her neck, the other moving up and down her back. This is madness, she thought deliriously, but if it be madness, let me never be sane again.

How long that kiss lasted she would never know, but the doctor's quiet "ahem" eventually separated them, and she knew from the amused gleam in his eye that he thought they were lovers. Her cheeks colored, and she turned away from both men for a moment, trying to school her passion-swollen features into a semblance of normality.

Jeremy steadied her with an arm around her waist, and it was Jeremy who asked the appropriate questions of the doctor and made the appropriate comments. Then, upon ascertaining that Christopher would not be conscious for several hours, he turned to Lindsey and said gently, "I'm taking you to dinner. We'll be back in plenty of time for you to be with Christopher when he wakes up. Knowing you, you haven't eaten anything at all today, and I know a delightful Chinese restaurant not far from here."

So, after weeks of separation, Lindsey found herself coupled with Jeremy once more. She had no time for preparation, no time to make sure her hair was just right or her makeup flawless. He just took her by the hand and led her out of the hospital as if he had the perfect right to do so, and Lindsey, fool that she was, let him. When Jeremy handed her gently into his silver Porsche, she knew what it was like to be a princess, beautiful, in love.

They arrived at the little Chinese restaurant in moments, and she discovered that everyone was dressed informally and the food was delicious.

"You're looking good," Jeremy said, after their food had been served.

"Thank you, kind sir," she laughed, knowing the absurdity of his compliment. She was wearing jeans and a fuchsia-colored blouse, chosen for comfort and hardly meant to cause a man to look twice. But Jeremy was looking...and looking. His dark eyes seemed black as they slowly inspected her. "I mean it, Lindsey. You look incredibly fresh and healthy."

"Yes, well, life has been a little more relaxed since our...business agreement," Lindsey acknowledged carefully.

"Ah, yes." Jeremy looked at her with a directness that took her breath away. "Our agreement. I think it's time you fulfilled your part of the contract."

"What do you mean?"

"You did promise to go out with me from time to time," Jeremy said calmly.

"Jeremy Boulanger, I promised no such thing, and you know it," Lindsey sputtered indignantly.

"What did you think I meant, then, Lindsey, when I said I wanted to continue seeing you?"

She looked away, and felt a faint pounding in her chest.

"What are you doing Friday night, Lindsey?" Jeremy continued softly.

"I'll be at the hospital," she managed coolly. "Christopher won't be released until next Tuesday or Wednesday."

"Wrong, Lindsey," Jeremy stated confidently. "Not about when Christopher will be released, but about what you're doing Friday night. You're going to spend it with me—I have two tickets to the new musical comedy that's downtown. Wait..." he cautioned, when she would have interrupted, "Christopher will be fine. We'll have dinner with him at the hospital, and the theater is close enough that we can check back with him after the performance."

"What about Catherine?" Lindsey continued to object.

"Get a baby-sitter, Lindsey."

She asked herself why she was bothering with so much resistance. Nothing would please her more than spending time with Jeremy, and she had not, after all, left either of her children with a sitter once since she had come to Chicago. "I'll ask around and see if I can find someone," she finally said.

After they had eaten, Jeremy took her back to the hospital and waited with her until Christopher woke up. Even through his postoperation fuzziness he was delighted to see Jeremy. "I thought..." he said, blinking, "thought you had forgotten—"

"No, son," Jeremy answered. "I promised I would take care of you, and I will. I was just giving your mother a little space, that's all."

Christopher closed his eyes before Jeremy was finished, and a small, contented smile played across the little boy's face. "Glad you're back," he said softly, before his even breathing indicated he was sleeping once more.

Jeremy sat with Lindsey for a little while longer. When it became apparent that Christopher was not going to waken soon, Jeremy stood and pulled Lindsey into his arms. "I think I've been away too long," he admitted ruefully. "I won't leave you again." Then he gave her a hard, possessive kiss that sent her senses reeling and her heart soaring.

Whatever Jeremy felt for her, this time she was not going to fight it. She would take one step at a time, but she would not run away like a frightened child.

Friday night Lindsey dressed carefully in a slim, long-sleeved black dress. The scoop neck and the low back showed off the perfection of her creamy skin. A wide silver belt emphasized her small waist, and a thick silver choke necklace brought out the color of her clear gray eyes. Dangling silver earrings with tiny diamond insets framed her face. She had swept her shoulder-length tresses up on the left side of her head and held them there with a black and silver comb. The only bright color Lindsey wore was in an oversized red silk rose, pinned high on her left shoulder, accompanied by matching red lipstick.

It was the most sophisticated look she had attempted in a long time, and she hoped Jeremy would approve of her efforts. That he was pleased was apparent by the sudden light leaping in his eyes when he came to her home to pick her up, and a murmured "You're beautiful, Lindsey," raised her spirits yet higher.

After kissing Catherine good night and checking to make sure the new baby-sitter understood her responsibilities, Lindsey left with Jeremy in plenty of time to share a take-out dinner with Christopher at the hospital.

Later, as they entered the theater, Lindsey knew she had never been so happy in her life. It was as if she were given an evening out of time, away from all the cares and worries that had plagued her since she was a very young girl. Jeremy aimed no barbed comments her way, and she in turn allowed him to see a warmth of spirit that he had so far been denied. His attentions were markedly possessive. His hand was constantly at her elbow, on her arm, pressed into the small of her back. And where his hands could not go, his eyes did, as he watched, as one bewitched, her lips as she talked and smiled, her eyes as they shone, her hair as it bounced and curled around her face. Many women eyed Lindsey enviously, for Jeremy Boulanger was a devastatingly handsome man obviously besotted with the slender woman at his side.

Lindsey bloomed. She didn't stop to question the change that had occurred between her and Jeremy. She only knew the play was funnier, the colors brighter, the actors the most talented of any she had ever seen. All of which was amazing since she couldn't seem to understand what the play was about. It was simply too hard to concentrate when Jeremy kept playing with her fingers, when the woodsy cologne he was wearing filled her nostrils, when his lips kept brushing her ear. She could hear his quiet breathing more clearly than she could hear the words of the lighthearted comedy.

Her dove-gray eyes sparkled as she looked his way. Was it possible she had ever sworn to be immune to his looks? She was sure she had never seen anyone so handsome. Still, through the love-clouded haze that had once been Lindsey's brain, a bell sounded. It was clear, ringing an unmistakable note of warning, and somewhere far away Lindsey made note of it, tucking the warning away for examination at a saner, clearer time.

During the intermission Jeremy ran into several people he knew. He would introduce Lindsey, his voice calm and steady, as "his special friend," or "my dear friend, Lindsey Wiltse," or simply as "my friend," and all the time his hand was possessively curved around her waist or resting on the small of her back. Lindsey could not remember a time when she had felt such a joyous sense of belonging.

Jeremy and Lindsey were standing together, each with a soft drink in hand, when a loud male voice called out, "Jeremy, old man!" She looked up to see a large, expensively clothed man making his way toward them. Jeremy's arm once again found its way around her waist.

"Bill..." Jeremy inclined his head.

"You're looking younger than ever, you rascal," the fair-haired man, who was in his mid-fifties, said genially. There was a question in his hazel eyes as he asked, "And this is . . . ?"

"Lindsey Wiltse," Jeremy offered without hesitation. "Lindsey, this is an old friend and business associate of mine, Bill Abbott."

Lindsey's smile froze on her face as the smiling man took her hand in his. A tall, willowy blonde moved to stand by Bill. "And this is my daughter, Lucille," Bill said proudly.

A strangely intense look was exchanged between Lucille and Jeremy, before he switched his gaze to Lindsey, watching her with suddenly wary attention.

Lucille Abbott was even more beautiful than her pictures. Her green silk dress and skillful makeup highlighted the most striking emerald eyes Lindsey had ever seen. Lucille's short, upswept hairstyle, her graceful posture, her perfectly molded features combined to give an unmistakable impression of elegant boarding schools and cool sophistication.

Lindsey was momentarily stunned into speechlessness.

For a moment the four of them stood there. It was Lucille who broke the silence. Her gaze running over Lindsey in swift appraisal, she said, "Jeremy has told me so much about you, Lindsey. How is your little boy?"

Jeremy had talked with Lucille about her? She discovered that pain, sharp and quick, could cut just as deep when delivered in a well-modulated, concerned tone as any other.

"Christopher is doing very well," Lindsey managed quietly.

The conversation continued to flow around her, not needing her participation. She stood and listened, and watched.

She is so beautiful, so fine, Lindsey thought. How can he not be in love with her?

"And how is your father, Jeremy?" Lucille was asking with refined solicitude. "Is he any better?"

"He is doing as well as can be expected," Jeremy answered briefly. Lindsey tensed beside him. Everything was suddenly back in perspective.

Jeremy had not mentioned his father since their first conversations in Michigan, and it came as a shock to her to remember that Jeremy must have been in touch with his father often during the past months. Had they discussed her, their little special project?

The houselights began to blink, and Jeremy and Lindsey separated from the Abbotts. Jeremy gave her an all-embracing look before helping her to her seat. The lights dimmed, and the play resumed.

When Lindsey had first met Jeremy, she had recognized at once that he was used to moving in circles where she might feel out-of-place and uncomfortable. Now, after seeing him next to Lucille and her father, she reminded herself of some cold, unalterable truths.

For instance, of course Jeremy was in touch with his father. She had somehow divorced Jeremy from the older man in her mind, and now she saw her mistake—they were father and son, intertwined for life, and if she loved one, she must of necessity accept the other.

Again she vowed to keep her distance. She must not love Jeremy Boulanger. Self-preservation demanded that she protect herself from such folly.

It would be best not to accept any more dates with Jeremy. She would get their relationship back on a business-like footing.

Jeremy shifted in his seat and placed his arm loosely around Lindsey's shoulders, and she closed her eyes against the torment. The play that had seemed so delightful only a short while before, now became an agony to be endured. She tried to concentrate on what was happening on the stage, but she found it increasingly difficult, especially when Jeremy began a gentle massage of her shoulders and neck. She thought she would die from the effort of blocking out the wonderful sensation that his touch aroused.

Sometime later she felt a gentle nudge. "Play's over." Jeremy was watching her unsmilingly. "Where have you been?"

"Oh!" she said, hating the break in her voice. "I guess my mind was wandering."

"I guess," Jeremy confirmed tersely.

She looked at him warily. "Actually," she said, "I've picked up a killer of a headache. Maybe you should just take me to the hospital, and I could take a taxi home."

"Not on your life, Lindsey," he said quietly. "I know you too well not to know when you're lying. You don't have a headache. And judging by the mulish expression on that lovely, stubborn face, you're not about to tell me what's really wrong, either."

Gone was the magic of the evening, the almost unbelievable closeness, the breathless awareness of each other. In silence, they filed out of the theater and walked to Jeremy's car.

The ride to the hospital was a short one. After a quick check with Christopher, who was sleeping contentedly, Jeremy and Lindsey headed home. It was a quiet ride, filled with a wary tension that Lindsey had no idea how to dispel. As they pulled up in her driveway, Lindsey was so locked in her misery that it took a few seconds for her to notice that a strange car was parked there. Jeremy was looking at her mockingly. "Expecting company?" he drawled.

She recognized the Pennsylvania license plates at the same time that she understood the meaning of Jeremy's rude insinuation, and she went white at the double blow.

"What is it, Lindsey?" Jeremy asked in a low, terse voice. "What's wrong now?"

She could only shake her head as she got out of his car. Without waiting to see if he followed her, she started up her front steps. An icy premonition seized her, numbing her of all feeling. Desperately she tried to pull herself together, knowing that no matter how wearing the evening had been so far, the worst was yet to come. She let herself in her house quietly.

The teenage baby-sitter she had hired was gone. Corrinne Wiltse was sitting on her sofa, and Bradley's brother, James, was right next to her. For a long moment Lindsey simply stood and stared at them; then, without a word of greeting passing her lips, she turned to go to Catherine's room. She wanted to see for herself that her daughter was all right.

"Catherine is sleeping just fine," Corrinne said in her most gracious lady-of-the-manor voice. "I thought about waking her up, but decided that tomorrow morning will do. Tonight you and I have things to discuss—oh!" Corrinne gave a little gasp of simulated surprise as Jeremy entered the room. "You must be Jeremy Boulanger. I'm so glad to meet you. I'm Corrinne Wiltse, and this is my son, James. We've come to get the children, you know. You have certainly helped me immensely. It really was too careless of Lindsey to allow you to spend that week in Traverse City. But, really, that can all be water under the bridge. There's no reason for your name to be brought up in court, is there? In fact—" Corrinne waved an exquisitely manicured hand "—I'm sure that after tonight Lindsey will understand that it is in the best interests of everyone concerned that she give custody of my grandchildren to me. Tell me, where is Christopher, Lindsey?"

Lindsey felt very, very tired. She had felt safe again, for a little while. She had allowed her defenses to weaken, and now Corrinne had taken her by surprise. "He's at the hospital. He's had his surgery, which was successful, Corrinne."

"So you managed it after all," Corrinne said in her cultured tones. "I congratulate you. I'm surprised you aren't spending the night there, but I suppose an evening on the town was more important than a night spent in a hospital room with your son."

Lindsey was barely listening to Corrinne's unfair accusation. From somewhere deep inside her she was finding the strength to fight again. Corrinne could do nothing tonight, of that she was sure. As far as Lindsey could tell, she had no legal papers, nor was she accompanied by anyone with authority.

"Why are you here, Corrinne? Why did you come tonight?" she asked, and the old insolent self-confidence was in her voice. She did not see how Jeremy had placed himself against the doorjamb so that he could observe the drama being played out in front of him. In fact, she had actually forgotten that Jeremy was even there, that at one time he had promised to protect her from Corrinne. She was so used to fighting her battles alone, and she was so unsure of Jeremy's feelings toward her, that in this moment he simply didn't count. She spared one quick glance at James, who sat awkwardly next to Corrinne, his face flushed in embarrassment. He, too, was unimportant. She clamped her eyes on her mother-in-law.

"I've come to make you one last offer before this goes to court," Corrinne said. "I am making this effort for the sake of the family name, and for the sake of my grandchildren, who would only suffer if the newspapers got wind of this situation.

"I have enough on you, now, Lindsey, to prove several times over that you're an unfit mother. The court will be very interested, not only in the week Mr. Boulanger spent with you in Traverse City, but also in the fact that he's paying your bills now. He's supporting you completely, my dear Lindsey. How does it feel to be kept?"

Corrinne paused and delicately lifted a lacy handkerchief to her lips. "I must say your behavior has not surprised me in the least. I always knew you were...cheap."

Corrinne smiled, a catlike smile of triumph. "There is no way you can keep the children now. My lawyers tell me that we are in absolutely no danger of losing this case. So I am offering you for the last time, a hundred thousand dollars to avoid a costly court case, which you cannot win, to sign over custody of the children to me." She turned to her red-faced son. "Do you have the papers, James?"

Lindsey had never felt such anger in her life, but it was a kind of conquering anger, a fierce blood-pounding anger that kept her mind calm and her expression under control. She knew that she would never, ever, give the custody of her children over to this cold, calculating woman. Corrinne's class-consciousness had destroyed her own sons, and her overbearing snobbishness would undoubtedly twist the precious son and daughter that were all that Lindsey had left of her and Bradley's loving.

Words began to pour from her mouth. "You are crazy, Corrinne, flat out crazy if you think that I would ever give up my children, whom I love, to be raised by a person like yourself. I almost feel sorry for you. I do. You are under several delusions, not the least of which is that your money and status make you more fit to raise Catherine and Christopher than I, even though I am their mother and I love them.

"But love is something you cannot buy, so you know nothing about it, Corrinne. Bradley certainly never received any of that commodity from you. You made it impossible for him to have any kind of decent relationship with a mature, self-confident woman. I see that clearly now."

Lindsey paused, took a deep breath and continued. "Bradley saved my life, and for that I am grateful, but I know for certain that you destroyed his. You will never know how much he wanted the love and open approval of his parents. Bradley was strong in some ways, and weak in others. Just like James here, who is completely humiliated by your lack of humanity, but too terrified to stand up for himself and live his own life.

"Do you think I want my children to be raised like that, Corrinne? I will never let you have them. I will fight you in court. As for Jeremy," she acknowledged his presence for the first time, "he and I are not and have never been lovers. I was sick that week in Traverse City, Corrinne. I had no one to help me, certainly not my Philadelphia relatives. The doctor's records will verify my truthfulness. I had pneumonia. Jeremy was there as a friend only, taking care of me and my children. And all the money that he has loaned, yes, loaned to me, has been legally documented. I am not being kept. Rather I am being helped through college. That should impress any judge, especially when I explain that you, with your millions, could have done the same thing, but would not. So take me to court, and see what happens."

"That won't be necessary." Jeremy's strong male voice startled them all. He continued to lean negligently against the living room doorjamb, but there was something in his posture that threatened menacingly. "All of what Lindsey has told you is true, Mrs. Wiltse, but what she hasn't told you is that I'm marrying her."

Lindsey didn't know who was more shocked, Corrinne or herself. Jeremy didn't even look at her as he continued sardonically, "You will agree, as the children's grandmother, that our marriage offers the perfect solution. The children already love me. I will be a good father to them. In addition, I have substantial money of my own. Catherine and Christopher will have everything you could have bought for them, and some things you could not: their own mother raising them, with a husband at her side."

Jeremy paused, then continued with deadly emphasis, "I think you might want to reconsider your threats, Mrs. Wiltse."

Corrinne had collapsed against Lindsey's sofa. Out of a face grown white and aged, her eyes glittered her hatred.

Jeremy came to stand by Lindsey, and he put his arm around her in a familiar gesture of support.

"I think it's time you and your son left, Mrs. Wiltse," Jeremy said softly, with just the barest thread of steel-edged determination in his voice. "You have bothered Lindsey long enough. Do not ever try to do so again. If you so much as darken her doorstep I'll have the best lawyers in the country draw up a lawsuit so long and involved that it will be years before the Wiltse name is out of the papers. You have my word on it."

Chapter Nine

Corrinne and James had left. Jeremy was messing about in her kitchen, making the inevitable cup of coffee. Lindsey sat in the old comfortable easy chair that she had brought with her from Michigan, her feet drawn up under her in the posture of a child. Jeremy walked out of the kitchen, bringing her a cup of steaming coffee. "Here," he urged. "Drink it."

Lindsey looked at Jeremy out of dove-gray eyes that had gone dull, listless. She made no move to accept the proffered cup.

Jeremy slid her a cool glance before setting the coffee cup on the table next to Lindsey's chair. He hunkered down on the carpet in front of her, so that his eyes were on a level with hers. She retreated into the chair, tears of bitter resentment stinging her eyes.

"Hey," Jeremy said gently, tenderly. "What is it? You look like a wounded kitten."

"I am not going to marry you," Lindsey said, her voice flat, hard.

"Why not? Our union would certainly solve all your problems."

"Not all of them," she said crossly. "Anyway, marriage is not a solution to anything." Her eyes flashed at him resentfully. "Bradley thought the same thing. He would marry me and solve all my problems. Well, I am sick and tired of being a problem for some man to solve. I can handle my own life. I do not need you to marry me. I was doing just fine with Corrinne before you butted in with your grand gesture."

"My grand gesture? Is that what you think? You are a fool, Lindsey Wiltse."

"Thank you so much for your statement of confidence," she replied caustically.

Jeremy rocked back on his heels. "You are the most stubborn woman I have ever met," he said with exasperation. "You deliberately misunderstand everything. Don't you want to be married? What's wrong with you, anyway? What about Christopher and Catherine? Children need a father, no matter how capable their mother is, and they could do a lot worse than have me. I genuinely like your children, Lindsey. I plan on learning to love them, just as I will love the children we will make together."

Lindsey was fighting for every ounce of composure she possessed. "You seem so sure of yourself," she said, her gray eyes snapping. "But you don't have the slightest inkling of what you're talking about. How do you know what my children will like or what they need? You have played benevolent uncle with them now and again, when it suited your purpose to do so. You have absolutely no idea of what being a parent entails."

"So enlighten me, if you can."

"Gladly," she countered. "Gladly, and then I never want you to mention marriage to me again.

"I'll tell you what being a father means," Lindsey began. "It means being on duty all the time, not just a week here and there when it suits you. It means when you're all

set to go on vacation, you stay home instead because someone has got the measles or the chicken pox, or is running a
fever. It means getting up in the night to calm a crying child
who has had a nightmare, or who is scared of things that
you can't even begin to comprehend.

"Being a father, Jeremy—" she thrust a pointing finger
at him, "—means being available when being available is
not convenient." She gave a ragged laugh.

"You say you want children? Why? Because you want to
see yourself perpetuated in another face, another little body
that looks like yours? Well, it's not enough." She leaned
forward in her chair, her voice low and intense. "Do you
know what kind of a world you're bringing children into?
Do you know what they're going to have to face growing up
in this world where everything is topsy-turvy? Do you understand that the commitment it takes to have children is
greater than any commitment you made to your career? Do
you understand that no success in the world can compen-
sate for failure in the home?"

Jeremy was studying her with unwavering regard. "Yes,"
he said, speaking slowly. "That's the kind of father I want
to be, and that's the kind of attitude I want the mother of
my children to have."

She glared at him speechlessly.

He reached out and took her hand, pulling her up out of
the chair and over to the sofa so that she could sit by him.

"Lindsey, Lindsey," he murmured. He put his arms
around her, and then directed her hand onto his chest, where
she could feel the steady beat of his heart. "Do you feel
that, Lindsey?" he asked hoarsely. "That is a heart, a
physical heart beating in a physical body. I am a human
being, not some monster of your imagination, waiting only
to fail you. Neither am I perfection, the perfect lover that
exists only in fairy tales. I am not your father, or mine. I am
not Bradley Wiltse. I am me, and I tell you now that I want
to marry you."

He tightened his hold when she would have shifted. "I do not know whether or not I can be a good husband, for I have never been one. I do not know that I will be an excellent father, but I can sure as hell try. I could give you my résumé and my statement of net worth, and you would see that I have been successful in many ways. For most women, that success alone would be enough for them to take a risk on me."

He laughed, a low sound of self-mockery. "It would have been enough for Lucille Abbott." He looked at her measuringly. "I could tell what you were thinking tonight when you met Lucille. But she's known for some time that my interest lay elsewhere." He smiled thoughtfully. "Only you didn't know, Lindsey. You've been so unaware of your own appeal, and so unimpressed by me. I think the reason you attracted me in the first place is that all of the outward stuff is not enough for you. When I told your mother-in-law I was going to marry you, I meant it, not for any of the reasons that you think, but because I have never found anyone I respect and admire as much as I do you."

Lindsey turned to him, her eyes wide and questioning, her lips trembling with confusion. He laid her hand back on her lap and moved his until it was covering her left breast. She felt his warmth through the sheer material of her dress, and breathed in sharply.

He smiled in acknowledgement. "Do you feel that, Lindsey Wiltse? Do you feel your senses leap and stir as I do? That is also important. I want you, and I know you want me. I want to make love with you, badly."

Lindsey was trembling all over now. He was right, she did want him, with every bit of life that was in her. Still, she fought his logic and conclusions. "Is that all there is, Jeremy? Wanting and respecting? Is that enough?"

His strong, warm hand had been encircling her breast with seductive, loving movements. He shifted her body so that he had freer access to what he desired, as he considered her question and its implications.

"You want me to say that I love you," Jeremy said with familiar insight. "I don't know if I can say those words and be honest, and I will not lie to you. The closest thing I can offer is the knowledge that ever since I met you I have not been able to get you out of my mind. Which is probably what my father had in mind when he sent me to you."

Lindsey turned so that she could see Jeremy's face. "And that's another thing," she said anxiously. "I don't know if I can ever face your father. I know I told you that I no longer hated him, but as long as we're being honest I might as well admit that I'm afraid I was lying. I do hate him. How can I marry you and hate your father?"

Jeremy's hand stilled against her neck, his thumb lay warmly across her jaw. She was experiencing that peculiar tightness of breath that his closeness had generated in her from the very beginning. She felt him sigh.

"You don't hate my father as he is now, Lindsey. You hate a memory. I never thought I would ever be defending my father to you, but I know you have only to meet him to dispel the awful memories you have."

"Do you love your father, Jeremy?"

His arms came around her, hugging her close to him, and she thought for a minute that he was not going to answer. His voice, when it came, was suspiciously husky. "Six months ago I would only have laughed in response to that question. Now . . . he's changed, Lindsey."

"Do you love him?"

"He's an old son of a gun, but I believe I do."

"And yet you really want to marry me?" she whispered.

He stroked her face gently with his hand, and she turned her head so that she could kiss his palm. "Yes," he answered gently. "That is what I want."

Her trembling and breathlessness increased. She felt as though all her air were in her throat, all her blood in her heart. She loved him, and he wanted to marry her. *She loved him.* Who was she to deny him? She wanted only to please him. Maybe their marriage would have a chance, after all. She could love enough for two.

He turned her face so that it tilted upward to meet his, then his lips were fused with her own in a kiss of such tenderness that she was sure she would melt on the spot. She felt herself falling helplessly as a free-flying bird might fall to the earth when it has been shot by a hunter. She could no more deny him than she could deny her own being, and she kissed him back fully, her hands reaching out to touch him, to encourage him in his ownership of her.

She was gasping and crying his name when he withdrew from her suddenly, leaving her hungry and aching. Satisfaction gleamed in his dark eyes.

"Marry me," he ordered softly, "as soon as it can be arranged."

"Yes," she moaned. "Oh, yes."

His hands were on her dress, but instead of unclothing her, he was straightening her shoulder where the material had slipped down rakishly. "Good," he elucidated victoriously. "This will wait until then, Lindsey."

She could only stare at him, wanting him so badly it was a physical agony. She had no willpower left. She supposed she should be glad that he had some.

Now that Jeremy had Lindsey's agreement, he gave her no chance to change her mind. He pulled strings, arranged schedules, gave orders, all with the ease of long practice, so that he and Lindsey could be married the following Wednesday evening. Christopher would come home from the hospital the previous day.

He said they would be married in the living room of her home. Only, he explained carefully, it was really his home, too, since he had bought the house in March, when she had committed to coming to Chicago.

She was not surprised.

He asked if she wanted to invite anyone.

She couldn't think of anybody.

Did she want a new dress?

She didn't think so.

Since Christopher was still recuperating, it would be best if they postponed their real honeymoon until later, he said.

That was fine with her.

Everything was fine. Let Jeremy make all the decisions. Let the days pass quickly. Let the protective numbness that was wrapping her in its sheltering darkness never go away.

She had never been so scared in her life.

Jeremy arranged to have his best friend, Tom Delancey, along with Tom's wife, Belinda, act as witnesses. Tom, a redheaded extrovert, was as much a surprise to Lindsey as she was to him.

"I never thought Jeremy would ever tie the knot," Tom said to her minutes before the ceremony. "You must be some special lady."

She smiled at him gratefully, trying not to let her confusion show.

"She is special," Jeremy said, joining them. "More special than she knows."

She looked at her children, sitting side by side on the sofa, silly expressions on their faces.

They had been ecstatic, of course. "I knew it, I knew it," crooned Catherine, when Jeremy had broken the news to the children while they visited with Christopher at the hospital, and Christopher had smiled happily. "Will you live with us now?" he asked.

"You bet," Jeremy answered easily. "All the time."

All the time. Jeremy Boulanger in her home, in her bed, in her life, all the time.

The white-haired minister was mercifully brief as he performed the ceremony. In no time the vows had been spoken, the obligatory kiss given, and Jeremy's ring had been placed on her finger.

Too late. It was too late. She had really done it. She was tied to this dark-haired man for life, and he had never once said he loved her. But she had said the words, made the promises, and was irrevocably committed.

And now she was a Boulanger, the greatest irony of all.

Tom and Belinda stayed to help with Christopher and Catherine. In no time the children were in bed, smiling and laughing and saying good-night to their new "Daddy." A few minutes later, obviously believing it was the tactful thing to do, the Delanceys said their goodbyes.

The house was quiet. Everything was cleaned up. There was nothing left with which to keep her hands busy.

She stood and stared out the window. It was past ten o'clock, and summer dusk cast its earthy glow on their quiet street. She rubbed her hands over her arms.

She felt Jeremy's fingers on her shoulders. He pulled her back against his tall, strong frame.

"Regrets, Lindsey?"

She didn't know what she thought. She resented the question. She wanted him to take charge, so that she didn't have to think or make any judgments for herself.

"Maybe I pushed too hard? Maybe the wedding was not how you wanted it?"

"The wedding didn't make any difference, Jeremy. It was short and sweet, and the children liked it," she said flatly.

"The children liked it," he mimicked her solemn tone. "Well, that's good. I'm glad someone is happy."

He turned her suddenly cold body so that she was facing him. He took in her bloodless, pinched face, her strained eyes. Placing his hands underneath her hair at her neck, he brought her head to rest on his shoulder. He gave a low, unbelieving laugh. "I think you're scared, Lindsey."

There was little sense in trying to hide it from him now. "Yes," she mumbled against his chest. It was incredibly foolish to feel this way. After all, she had been married before.

Jeremy's right hand began a slow movement up and down her back. For a long time they stood there, unspeaking, his hand moving in a relaxing rhythm, assuaging her fear.

"Let's sit down, Lindsey," he said at last.

He handled her like fragile porcelain. Carefully he settled her on the sofa. Solicitously, he tucked a light yellow blanket around her. He shrugged out of his suitcoat, loosened his tie, then settled his own weight next to hers. He brought his arm around her shoulders, and again brought her head to rest against his chest.

She resisted nothing, and gave nothing.

But she was beginning to feel again. She felt the fabric of his fine white silk shirt, and remembered that everything Jeremy owned was the very best. She felt the movement of his chest as he breathed easily, and thought of his beautiful, well-disciplined body.

And she was... just Lindsey. Lindsey Wellington. The girl nobody wanted. The little girl who never grew up.

And now this perfect specimen of manhood had married her, was going to make love to her, and he would find out just how imperfect she was. She wished, childishly, that she could run away.

Jeremy was dropping kisses on her head, and his arms surrounded her comfortingly. She remembered the message from months ago: *I will comfort your body and your heart. Let me. Let me.*

At last Jeremy spoke. "I don't know much about this kind of relationship, Lindsey, but if it helps, I'm scared, too. After tonight, after we spend time in our bed, things will be different between us. I am giving you power to bring me pain."

His words surprised her. "I don't understand."

"I don't either, but I know it's true. Up until now, it's been a kind of game, an illusion. But now, the illusion is over. Only reality remains. And reality is you and me together, Lindsey. I'm going to make love with you, and when we're done, you will have power over me. I give you that. I trust you with it, knowing that you will use it to give me pleasure, but also there is the risk that you will cause me pain.''

She didn't like what he was saying. She didn't want to hurt him. She didn't want to hurt anybody.

Yet it was so true. The hardest blows she had ever received had been given by those she loved the most.

''Is life always like this, Jeremy?''

''I don't know. I'm just learning, too, Lindsey. We're equals, right now.''

His lips touched hers in a feather-light kiss. With her hand up, she brought his head down more firmly so she could kiss him back. She felt her fear receding.

''I hope....'' Her voice trailed away uncertainly.

''What, Lindsey?''

''I hope I don't...disappoint you.''

''You will not disappoint me.'' The light summer blanket had slipped down, and Jeremy began slowly unfastening the tiny pearl buttons down the front of her sapphire blue dress. She shivered against him and his hand slid beneath the fabric of her dress to rest against her rose pink silk undergarments.

''How do you know I won't?'' she asked tremulously. ''I don't know it myself. I don't think I'm very good at this at all.''

''Lindsey, you can't disappoint me. I have no expectations at all right now. But I know some things that you don't, apparently. I know you're beautiful. Exquisitely beautiful. I am so proud to have you in my life.''

He shifted her against him, and his hand began to work its own brand of comfort against her silk-clad skin.

''I'm not going to leave you, Lindsey. No matter what happens tonight, or next month, or next year. I'm not going to leave you.''

Wonderful words. Marvelous, bittersweet words. She swallowed against a sudden, painful swelling in her throat.

She thought of Bradley. "You can't know that," she said, harshly bitter.

"Lindsey, don't you think I know what's happened to you these last few days? You left me, Lindsey. You shut yourself off. You have to stop doing that. There can be no barriers between you and me tonight. You will have to open yourself to me, Lindsey. You will have to risk being hurt, in order to taste the pleasure."

She wanted to. She wanted to.

He slipped her arms out of her dress, and the fabric slithered in soft folds to her waist.

"I like your silk slip, Lindsey. I like your lacy bra. But I like your smooth skin most of all."

His lips touched her neck, her throat, the curve of each breast. "Do you feel the pleasure, Lindsey?"

"Yes." Her reply was short and breathless, and filled with need.

"I won't leave you."

"Oh, Jeremy."

Again, he pulled her head against his chest. One hand played with the strap of her slip, his fingers sliding up and down the thin piece of material, his knuckles rubbing against her skin.

"Now, I'm going to tell you what I'm going to do. I'm going to carry you to that bed down the hall and lay you on it. Then I'm going to finish undressing you very carefully. I'm going to undress myself, and we will be naked before each other. And just as I will give you power over me, you will give me that same power. You will trust me, Lindsey. You will trust my hands, that they will not hurt you. You will believe my lips when they tell you how beautiful you are. You will trust my eyes, and when they darken with passion and need for you, you will believe that, too."

"Yes," she said.

"Touch me, Lindsey. Touch me now."

She reached out her hand to touch his face. Like a blind person, she memorized the feel of his features through her fingertips. She brought her fingers to his lips. He closed his eyes, and kissed the soft pad of each one. She began to tremble.

"More," he ordered softly. "Touch me more."

Tentatively, she brought her hand down on his chest, then lower to his thigh. She began to rub softly.

"Ahh," he groaned lightly. "Ahh, Lindsey. You are so desirable. You are so beautiful. Of all women, you are the most desired."

She didn't know what to say.

"Tell me, Lindsey. Tell me that you know how desirable you are."

"Jeremy..."

"Tell me, Lindsey."

She thought it was a game, so she began lightly enough, "I know..." She stopped, and found she could not continue. Her hand lay suddenly still against his leg.

"You are, Lindsey. You are desirable. Tell me."

"I know that..." She buried her head in his chest.

"Say it, Lindsey."

Cruel torture. But with all her heart, she wanted to say the words. Yet years of self-doubt closed her lips more surely than any physical binding ever could. Jeremy continued to play with her slip strap. With the thumb of his other hand he began to outline the shape of her lips.

"I'm waiting, Lindsey," he said. "We stop right now unless you say it."

Slow tears ran their inevitable course down her face. She asked, "Do you really think I'm desirable, Jeremy?"

"There is no doubt, Lindsey." His voice held hidden laughter.

"Then I will say it," she got out at last. She laughed shakily. "I know that I am ... desirable."

"And you're beautiful. Say it."

It was easier this time.

"I know that I am beautiful."

Unbelievable lightness. Incredible relief. Joy. I am. I am. Beautiful and desirable and worthy. Thank you, Jeremy. Thank you for knowing so much.

"Good," Jeremy said huskily. "So good. You're learning the truth about yourself, and your truth includes me, Lindsey."

"Oh, yes."

He smiled. "Do you know how you look, sitting here half-naked and trusting on my lap? You're radiant, Lindsey. You're all lit up and shining with the knowledge of your own power. I couldn't resist you if I wanted to." He took a deep, ragged breath. "I don't want to resist you anymore, Lindsey." His hands shifted, surrounded her face.

"Kiss me now," he demanded.

His mouth was open and hungry. The gentleness of a moment ago was gone, and so was her fear. He gave her power to hurt him. She was desirable. She had nothing to fear. She wanted him.

"Now, Lindsey," he said, his voice deep and shaking and full of promises. "Now we are going to that bed. And I'm going to love you, and you're going to hold nothing back. I'm going to love you all night long, Lindsey."

She didn't care that triumph as well as passion shone from his dark eyes. She didn't care that she was shaking uncontrollably, so that her own longing was plain for him to see.

Just for tonight, she would trust him. She would forget all her painful memories, all her unhealed wounds. She would see only the need in his eyes, and become for him what he most wanted: beautiful and desirable and womanly.

She would, at last, be herself.

Chapter Ten

Lindsey woke to find that Jeremy had already left their bed. She stretched languorously, sensuously. She turned and rubbed her hand lovingly across the pillow where Jeremy's head had rested. She realized she was already smiling. It was going to be a lovely day. She was sure that nothing could dim the happiness she felt. She was like a star whose light, long hidden, shone all the more brightly, as if to make up for years of darkness.

She drew on her robe, intent on finding Jeremy. She would just wish him a good morning before returning to shower and dress. But even as she buttoned her robe and tied its belt firmly around her waist, she knew that she was going to tell him much more than good morning. She was going to tell him that she loved him.

Predictably, she found Jeremy with the children in the breakfast room. Catherine and Christopher were still in their pajamas, and both of them had the look about them of the cat that swallowed the cream.

"Are you really our daddy now?" Catherine was asking Jeremy.

"Sure thing, honey," he answered her gently.

"I'm so glad," Catherine told him seriously. "I wanted you to be our daddy."

"Daddy, Daddy, Daddy," Christopher was singing in a decidedly off-key manner.

Then Jeremy saw Lindsey standing there. Immediately he rose and held a hand out to her. His eyes swept over her new dusky blue robe, took in her bare feet, and came back to rest on the tousled hair that she was holding back with one hand, before he looked into her luminous eyes.

A slow smile appeared on his face. "Good morning, Mrs. Boulanger," he said softly.

She was stepping toward him before she noticed his own apparel. He was dressed in the three-piece suit that was the uniform of his workplace. This one was gray, with tiny little red and white threads running through it. His hair was washed and combed, and he was freshly shaven.

"You're not going to work?" she asked, dismay evident in her tone, even as her hand reached out to grasp his.

His smile faded, and his eyes turned suddenly grave. "And if I am?" he asked expressionlessly.

Unutterable disappointment seized her, dimming her new-found light, making her suddenly tired and filled with dread. Was it truly possible that he was so unaffected by what had happened between them last night, that he could go about his daily business as if today were the same as yesterday? He looked unbelievably rested, fresh, cool as a summer shower, and she thought for a mad moment that he was going to place a chaste, unfeeling kiss on her cheek before heading out the door.

The words of love she had longed to say died a sure death as she stood there, looking at him blankly.

"Do you have to?" she asked tentatively, struggling against the sense of doom that was weighing heavily on her heart. "I thought . . . I'd hoped . . . we would spend the day together."

He stood towering over her, even as he tucked her hand in his arm and brushed his lips over her hair.

"You have yet to tell me how you feel about your new name, Mrs. Boulanger." His quiet voice held an undertone of bitterness.

What was wrong with him? Where had the tender, affectionate man of last night gone?

"I said the vows. I took the name," she responded huskily.

"But you hate it, don't you? I saw you wince when Belinda called you by my name."

Had she winced? She had been so enveloped in her own fears, she had been unaware that she had reacted at all.

Yet, last night . . . he had not been angry last night, only tender and loving and unbelievably, passionately hungry. And he had been so determined to make her forget all that had gone before. Now he seemed determined that she should remember. She was utterly confused as, with a wink to the children, he escorted her into the front living room.

"Jeremy, what's going on? Didn't last night mean anything to you at all?" she asked, a pleading, puzzled note in her voice.

"What was it supposed to mean?"

She turned her back on him, her shoulders proudly set, and strode back to the kitchen. "Catherine and Christopher," she said with parental authority to the two children who were watching them wide-eyed. "Go and get dressed now. We'll have breakfast shortly."

Keeping her back to Jeremy, she walked to the kitchen window that had been one of her favorite spots in her new home. Two old oaks stood towering in the backyard, a matched pair of aged, scarred survivors that had always been majestically beautiful to Lindsey. Now she fixed her eyes on them as the only stable things in a world that had begun to spin in a disturbingly disorienting manner.

Jeremy made no move toward her. Instead, she heard him take a seat at the breakfast table. Tears hovered perilously near.

At last he said, "Turn around, Lindsey."

She did as he asked, haughtily. Her eyes glistening with the effort of not weeping, she raised her chin and stared at him.

He took it all in, her stance, her grief-drenched eyes, her burgeoning anger. "I'm sorry," he said. "You deserve more than this."

But when he rose to pull her to him, it was with an unfamiliar roughness. He forced her face upward, so that her eyes were compelled to meet his.

"I'm not going to work, Lindsey."

"But you're all dressed . . ."

"I thought to deceive you, but I see now I was wrong to do so." He shrugged out of his suitcoat and laid it around a chair back. Watching Lindsey steadily, he removed his tie and loosened the top button on his shirt. "I'm going to visit my father, Lindsey. Just like I do every day."

"Your father . . ." she repeated vaguely.

"He lives two miles from here. It's one of the reasons I bought this place," he said.

But he had bought this home for her. He had told her so. She had believed that his father had nothing to do with it, had nothing to do with *them*. Now understanding dawned with all of its unpleasant clarity.

Blindly she found a chair and sat in it. "You bought this house because it was close to your father," she repeated slowly.

"And for you, Lindsey," he replied evenly.

She knew when she married him who his father was. She had known from the beginning. Why then did she feel this ache, this sense of betrayal? The fear that she was nothing more to Jeremy than a deathbed assignment filled her chest, making her feel painfully constricted.

"You planned all this, didn't you?" she lashed out wildly. "You never lost control or perspective for one minute, did you? You had it all arranged from the beginning, and you shared nothing of your plans with me. You just manipulated and controlled until you got what you wanted."

"You wanted it, too, Lindsey," he reminded her bleakly, his visage cold and pale. "Even if you never admitted it like I did, you wanted it at least as much."

"Do you talk to him about me?" she continued unreasoningly. "Do you tell him how successful you've been in carrying out his orders to help me? Of course you've told him that we're married." She took a deep breath. "But maybe our marriage was all his plan anyway?"

"The marriage was my idea, Mrs. Boulanger," he said curtly. He stood tall and rigid, the veins in his hands and neck dominant against his brown skin.

She had never seen him look so glacial, or so withdrawn.

She knew what it meant. He was hiding his feelings behind that wall of ice.

A tiny seed of shame began to grow in her heart. She was behaving badly, more than badly. A wedge was growing between them that would take major surgery to remove, unless she acted now.

Her voice was tight and small with her humiliation, but she made herself say the words. "I'm sorry," she apologized. "I'm wrong, I know it. Of course you must see him. You took me by surprise, that's all. You do have the habit of doing that. Of course you must continue to visit your father." She still could not look at him.

He sighed. "Lindsey, I visit my father every morning, just about the same time, because this time of the day is good for him. He's lucid, he has more strength." He paused briefly. "And he has less pain."

"You should have told me, Jeremy."

"You knew he was dying. You refused to see him. I would not go today except that I can't be sure that he will be alive tomorrow." He continued with brutal honesty, "It wasn't only for Christopher that I didn't want a honeymoon just now."

For a moment she didn't answer, as she absorbed the fact that he had hidden yet more motives from her.

"How...how long does he have?" she asked at last.

"Two or three months, maybe."

She could stand anything for three months. She could afford to be generous.

"Go see him, Jeremy. As often as you wish. I won't stand between you." She felt so much better now. She really wasn't so cruel and unfeeling as she had sounded a minute ago.

"Won't you come with me, Lindsey?" The plea seemed wrung from Jeremy, and for a moment she wavered.

But when her answer came, it was firm. "No, I would only upset him. I couldn't see him without remembering...without feeling...so bitter, so angry. I'm sure he doesn't need me reminding him of what he would rather forget."

"You share his name, Lindsey, as well as mine," Jeremy reminded her harshly. "You need to see him before he dies." He continued relentlessly, "He would like to meet your children. He's mentioned it, several times."

But he was asking too much. She shook her head sightlessly, trying not to see the accusation in Jeremy's eyes, trying to escape the feeling that she was failing him.

He stared at her expressionlessly for a moment longer, then bent and placed a hard, punishing kiss on her lips. "I'll be back in an hour," he said. "We'll talk then."

They did talk, but not about John Boulanger. And not about Lindsey's past. And, after one brief frustrating argument, not about her going to school in the fall, either.

"You'll change your plans about college, of course," Jeremy had stated with unqualified certainty.

"Why?" was her startled response.

"You don't need it, now. You don't have to prove anything to me. You have a family, and I will take care of you all."

"I won't change my plans," she told him stubbornly, appalled at how little they understood each other.

Jeremy took off the week and a half following their wedding, and the only time he spent away from his new family was the short while each morning when he went to see his father. And if he and Lindsey were not communicating well, he was wonderful with the children.

They went to the beach, to the park, to the movies, all the time being careful not to overtax Christopher's legs. Jeremy helped make the daily trips to the hospital required for Christopher's physical therapy.

Before the first week was done, Jeremy insisted that Lindsey hire a housekeeper. "You're going to be back and forth from the hospital," he stated. "And if you will insist on going to school in the fall, you'll need help at home," he had added darkly.

Two nights before Jeremy had to return to his office, Lindsey invited Tom and Belinda Delancey to a late-evening dinner. This allowed Lindsey to put her children to bed early, so that the four of them could have a quiet, relaxed time without the interruption of little voices, much beloved though they were.

Lindsey had prepared a roast with twice-baked potatoes, homemade bread, sugared carrots and green beans with slivered almonds. Everything was ready on time and tasted delicious. The Delanceys were lavish in their praise.

"You've got it all, Jeremy," Tom teased. "Beauty, family and domestic talent. No wonder you fell so hard."

Lindsey blushed at the praise, and Jeremy smiled crookedly. "My wife's talents are certainly numerous," he agreed, causing Lindsey to blush even further.

Belinda spoke enviously. "Don't think Tom's joking, Lindsey," she said. "We've tried and tried to have children, so Jeremy inheriting two as beautiful as yours has been just a little hard for me, especially, to take.

"Don't get me wrong," she continued as Jeremy would have spoken. "I'm happy for you, Jeremy. It's just that sometimes a career seems a poor second to motherhood—especially when you can't have it."

"Adopt," Jeremy suggested succinctly.

"We've already started proceedings," Tom nodded. "At last. We've been told it will probably take another six months or so."

The conversation changed course, and Lindsey was feeling relaxed and in control when the telephone rang. Jeremy answered its summons.

"Hello? Yes, Helen? Oh? How bad?" A silence fell as all four occupants of the room realized that something serious had happened. "I'll be right there."

When Jeremy turned to face Lindsey and their two guests, his face was ashen. "I've got to go," he said.

Lindsey looked at him in dismay but it was Tom who immediately came to the right conclusion: "Your father?"

Jeremy didn't look at Lindsey as he nodded, but Tom and Belinda did. Her hands clenched under the table as she saw Jeremy's pain, but she knew she had no comfort to offer him. Tom and Belinda obviously were waiting for her to offer to accompany her husband, but the words stuck in her throat. Jeremy turned abruptly to leave.

"I'll go with you," Tom offered, clearly perplexed by Lindsey's silence.

"Thanks." Jeremy's voice was strained.

It took only seconds before the two men were out the door and Lindsey was left alone with Belinda Delancey. Belinda was looking at Lindsey with disbelief.

"Why didn't you go with Jeremy?" she demanded. "It was your place as his wife."

Lindsey shrugged, and rose to begin clearing the dishes from the table.

"I thought more of you," Belinda continued, frankly angry. "I never thought you would let Jeremy go off by himself like that."

"Jeremy didn't ask me to go," Lindsey said calmly.

"Come on, Lindsey. I know something's wrong here. I've never seen Jeremy look so... hurt."

Hurt. She had hurt him. He had given her that power and she had used it. She had told herself that she loved him, but her love had been overpowered by her ancient hatred.

"John Boulanger is evil," she spat out at Belinda. "I couldn't stand to be in the same room with him. I'd feel... contaminated."

"You've got to be kidding. You talk like that about your own father-in-law?"

Lindsey knew that she did sound horrible. She could understand if Belinda was repelled.

"Belinda, let me tell you a story. It's not a pretty one, and it will take some time."

"I have all the time in the world, Lindsey," Belinda said, openly curious.

Lindsey told her everything, from the beginning, not finding it strange that she had now told her life story to two people, when she had not done so for years before.

When she was done, Belinda reached across to give Lindsey a hug.

"I like you, Lindsey," she said. "But you don't know the whole truth. Let me fill you in on some things.

"You really don't know your husband yet, as I do," Belinda said. "He and Tom and I grew up together. We were best friends for years, and as a result he and I talked a lot. He grew up feeling he wasn't wanted by his mother or his father. His mother was a beauty, all right, on the outside. She liked to play the field, and Jeremy remembers her taunting his father that she didn't know who his father really was."

"But that's impossible," Lindsey interrupted. "He looks just like John Boulanger."

"I know that, so would anyone with eyes in his head, but Jeremy himself couldn't see it until he was older. His parents divorced before he was eight, so those taunts formed an important part of his childhood memories."

Lindsey felt a sharp pain in the region of her heart. *How horrible for Jeremy. He deserved so much more.*

Belinda was not finished. "Then, just about the time that Jeremy was settling into college life, his father fell in love again—with your mother, and you know how that ended. John retreated into himself at a time when Jeremy was just trying his wings as a young man. He attempted to make overtures to his father, only to meet with complete indifference. I think Jeremy went a little crazy, then." Belinda looked at Lindsey, appealing for understanding. "Has Jeremy ever told you he loves you?"

Lindsey shook her head.

"I'm not surprised. I think your husband is afraid of love," she said gently. "I don't think he has ever received it, so he's unsure about how to give it. He will try, though. He'll show you in a million ways that he cares, but I've never heard him say the words to anyone."

She remembered Jeremy telling her he loved his father; a strange huskiness in his voice had accompanied his confession.

Lindsey sat silent for a moment, wrapped in her own thoughts. "I thank you for sharing this with me, Belinda," she said softly. "But I think perhaps this marriage was not such a good idea, after all. Jeremy's father is dying, and he will never forget that I would not go and see him."

"Then go. Fight for the future, don't live in the past."

Lindsey took a deep breath. "All right, I will. If he lives through the night, I will." Yet even as she said the words, she wondered where she would find the courage to live up to them.

* * *

Jeremy arrived home about 3:00 a.m. One look at his face told Lindsey that his father lived: there was no death-grief there. But Jeremy was exhausted.

"How is he?"

"Out of current danger," was his brief reply.

He was tired, so tired. He undressed and lay next to his wife, waiting for blessed sleep to overtake him.

"Turn over on your stomach, Jeremy," Lindsey ordered.

"What?"

"Turn over. I'll rub your back."

He shrugged, but did as she asked. Tentatively at first, and then with strong, firm hands, she massaged the tension from his neck and back. Five minutes passed, then ten. Still she kept at the loving motions. When thirty minutes had passed, she was sure he had faded into sleep, and she lay down beside him.

His arm snaked out to surround her body. Roughly he turned her face to his and ground his mouth against hers cruelly, angrily. She felt his desire to strike out, to punish; she understood his need to bury his grief.

But she would not be used. If he needed her in this way tonight, she would give as well as take. She reached up to tangle her fingers in his hair, then pulled his head back before kissing him with a hunger equal to his own.

She felt his surprise. Then, with a grunt, he shifted his body so that he was half covering her. His mouth devoured her own, even as his hands began to make ungentle demands on her body.

She held nothing back, as he had taught her. She was tired, too, and confused and frightened. She, too, needed the reassurance that their joining could bring.

Their hands and lips and bodies spoke wordlessly of the way they had hurt each other, of the grief and pain they were both still enduring, of the anger that raged beneath the surface. And when they were done, they lay, damp and exhausted, in each other's arms.

*   *   *

Three days after Jeremy returned to his office, the call from John Boulanger's doctor came. John was feeling much better. When he had heard that she had requested a time to see him, he had improved markedly. He could see her now.

Belinda, previously aware of Lindsey's plan, came quickly to the house to watch the children during Lindsey's visit.

Lindsey was ushered into John Boulanger's home by a uniformed nurse; she stood tensely in the doorway of his room as she was being announced. The room was strongly masculine: paneling covered the walls and parquet flooring was unsoftened by even a throw rug. There were three pictures on the wall opposite her: the first of an old farmhouse in a well-aged photograph, the second a group of people dressed in the styles of sixty years ago and obviously gathered together for a group portrait, the third a Model T.

"My first car," John Boulanger spoke from his bed, and she started in guilty surprise. "It was an antique even then. And the farm is where I was raised. The people are my family. I'm the shiny nosed kid on the left."

To fill in the sudden silence, she asked, "Was the farm close to Chicago?"

"No, North Dakota." He paused. "Turn around, Lindsey Wellington," he said, using her maiden name.

She did as he ordered, steeling herself for the feelings of bitter hatred she was sure would swamp her when she at last met the eyes of the man who had caused her so much pain so many years ago. But, astoundingly, the feelings didn't come. She didn't feel anything. She *saw* an old and dying man, with features that strongly resembled those of the man she loved. He was thin to the point of emaciation, but his eyes were as bright as ever.

"Come and sit by me, please. I want to see what Ruth Ann's daughter looks like, all grown up."

She moved awkwardly to the chair at his bedside, noticing for the first time the picture of her mother that was propped on his reading table. Her eyes widened as she took

in the picture, for this was a Ruth Ann that she had barely
known. This laughing-eyed, gay woman bore no resem-
blance to the shadow that had moved silently through
Lindsey's childhood. Without meaning to, she picked up the
picture. She realized with new insight how her shy, quiet
mother could be drawn to the man who would make her feel
like the woman in this picture. She felt the cursed, familiar
tears start behind her eyelids, and she wiped them away,
embarrassed. "She looks so happy here," she said.

"She was happy," John said gently. "Happy with me. I
loved her, Lindsey, and she loved me."

Lindsey could not look at the man in the bed beside her.

"What we did was wrong, I know that now. I've come to
regret what we did many times and in many different ways.
But our love was not wrong. It was the best thing that ever
happened to either of us. Only both of us were so new at
loving that we pretty near destroyed those around us whom
we cared the most about. It broke your mother's heart to
leave you behind, Lindsey. And it more than broke mine to
be the cause of her death."

Something inside her shattered. With a great sob she
turned away. The tears formed rivers down her cheeks. She
heard the old man shift in his bed; she felt his trembling
hand on her shoulder.

"I want you to know I'm sorry for everything, Lindsey.
Not a day has passed in the last fifteen years that I didn't
want to tell you that."

*He's a man. He's just a man. He's part of the human
condition, Bradley. You were right, in this you were right.*

"Thank you," she heard herself saying. "Thank you for
loving my mother." She turned, reached out and took his
frail hand in her young, strong one.

"Have you forgiven me, Lindsey?" he asked, his voice
hoarse and wavery.

Could she forgive John Boulanger? How could she not?
You don't hate my father, Lindsey, she heard Jeremy saying. *You hate a memory.* Memories swirled around her now.

Images of hearing news of her mother's death from her father's stricken lips, images of finding her father, dead, in his beloved truck. Images of foster homes and orphanages. Images of hate-filled years, of cold-shouldered rejections. They were old pictures, old burdens, and she saw, with a blazing beam of inner light, that those ancient images had been replaced by more recent ones. Scenes with Bradley, as he tried, in his own way, to give her the love and self-confidence she lacked. Pictures of Christopher learning to walk again, of Catherine loving school and people and life. Memories of Jeremy laughing with her, loving her.

It was a moment to be remembered forever, this feeling of sudden lightness, of rebirth, of transcendent love. Peace such as she had never known overflowed from her breast. She smiled at John Boulanger tremulously. She was still gripping his hand as the cleansing tears continued to run down her cheeks, and she was uncaring that he saw, uncaring that his eyes were unashamedly moist also. In a burst of pure affection she leaned down and kissed John Boulanger's leathery, withered cheek.

"Now," John Boulanger's frail voice took on a hint of his old authority. "Dry your tears. I want you to tell me everything..."

Hours later, Jeremy found her sitting by his father's bed. John was asleep, and Lindsey was resting, her head laid against the back of the wing chair next to his bed. She held John's hand in hers. Her face had a peacefulness in repose that was angelic in its purity.

He's made his peace.

As if she heard his thought, Lindsey's eyes flew open.

Hello, she greeted him silently. *I love you.*

He stared at her, mesmerized.

She drew her hand away from his father's. "Shh," she said. "He's sleeping."

"So I see." Jeremy's eyes flicked over his father expressionlessly. "I've come to take you home."

"What about my car?"

"Leave it here until tomorrow."

"Yes. All right."

When they were in the Porsche, she found the courage to tell him her heart for the first time. "I love you, Jeremy."

She thought at first that he had not heard her, until she noticed his whitened knuckles on the steering wheel. It made her sad, those white knuckles. "I'm sorry," she said softly.

With a curse he swung the car into their driveway.

"Sorry?" he demanded. "What for?"

She made a gesture with her hand that said, *everything*.

"Come with me," he barked. Obediently she followed him into their house, through the living room, down the hall, into their bedroom.

"Where are the children?" she asked, noticing the unnatural stillness.

"I had Belinda take them to her house," he replied tersely. "I needed to talk with you."

She sat on the bed, waiting.

He sat next to her.

"Thank you for visiting my father," he began.

"I should have done it long ago."

He took her hand, rubbed the top of her knuckles with his thumb in a gentle, back-and-forth motion. "Lindsey, I don't know how to tell you this," he said at last. "But I owe you an apology."

She turned to him, startled at the bleakness of his tone.

"You were right, what you said the morning after we were married. I planned all of this. Our marriage, your dependency on me. I did it as a favor to my father, no other reason."

She didn't want to hear this. Not any of it.

"He needed me, Lindsey. For the first time in my life, he needed me. I'm thirty-five years old, and, like a child, I wanted to please him."

"Don't, Jeremy. Don't tell me these things."

"I have to, Lindsey. I want to start over. I want you to forgive me, if you can. I want a real marriage."

"Jeremy, there is nothing to forgive."

"You don't understand," he said heavily.

"I understand more than you know," she replied. Slowly she began unbuttoning his shirt. "How long are the children going to be gone?"

"Until I call Belinda and Tom. What are you doing, Lindsey?"

"Touching you."

He closed his eyes briefly, then stilled her hands with his larger ones. "I don't deserve you. I don't deserve this."

"Do you know what, Jeremy? You're a big, bold man, but you're scared. Just as scared as I was on our wedding night." She freed her hands and reached for his last button. He was wearing a fine cotton undershirt, and she raised it over his stomach. She leaned over to kiss the taut muscles there.

"Tell me you love me, Jeremy."

"Lindsey, haven't you heard anything I just said?"

"I heard all of it. Tell me, Jeremy." She pulled the arms of his shirt, so he could draw himself out of it. Then she lifted his undershirt over his shoulders. How she loved his fine, firm body. How she loved everything about him.

"It would be a lie, Lindsey. I don't know what the word means."

She kissed him on his cheek, nibbled at the corner of his lip.

"I'll tell you what love means, Jeremy. It means the time you stayed with me in Traverse City, when I was sick and ungrateful and desperately needy.

"It means coming to me in the hospital when Christopher was having his operation.

"It means taking on the responsibility of children who you never fathered, and teaching them and helping them.

"It means marrying me, and helping me through that night after the wedding. It means revealing things about myself that I would never have dreamed.

"It means caring for a father who never showed you affection when you most needed it.

"You know how to love, Jeremy. You just need to say the words."

She began to unzip his pants.

He was breathing deeply, and she rested her hand on his thigh. "This feel good, Jeremy?"

"Sure. Sure it does, Lindsey."

"Then tell me."

"Lindsey..."

"Tell me, or this stops right now." She was laughing at him.

"I can't, Lindsey."

"Repeat after me: I love you, Lindsey."

She thought at first he would not do it. She felt his stomach tighten, his breathing grow more shallow. She continued to plant little kisses all over his body.

All the time she loved him. She willed him the courage to say the healing words.

When his voice came, it was no more than a humble whisper.

"Ahh, Lindsey. I love you. I do."

She looked up then, and saw the unmistakable moisture in his eyes.

She smiled at him radiantly. "And I love you, and I am desirable, and right now..."

"Yes?"

"This desirable woman desires you."

Later that night, after the children were asleep, and Tom and Belinda had left, they lay next to each other in their bed, holding hands, and talked of old hurts and new dreams.

"I think I loved you from the first moment I saw you," Jeremy told Lindsey huskily. "You were so brave and angry and beautiful. I'm sorry it's taken me so long to say the words. I was sure that I had lost you before I realized what I had."

Lindsey listened, content, feeling warm and loved and cherished and safe.

"Why don't you want me to go to school, Jeremy?"

He reached over to stroke her hair. Then he sighed, a wistful, longing sigh. He kissed her, a tiny butterfly kiss that left soft promises in its wake. His answer came in the form of another question. "Don't you want any more babies, Lindsey?"

She twisted on the bed so that she could see his face. "Babies?" she asked.

"I'm thirty-five," he told her. "I'd like to father children of my own."

"Okay," she agreed happily. "Let's get pregnant."

"Don't tease me about this, Lindsey." He looked incredibly stern.

She started to laugh, and the sound of it startled him. His face began to turn a dull red before she realized her mistake. "Jeremy," she said. "What fools we have been. I'd love to be pregnant. I have never had a greater experience than giving birth to Christopher and Catherine. Not even..." She added mischievously, "with you."

"But your education—"

"Can be worked around. We can compromise, Jeremy. I'm willing to bend, if you are. I know myself well enough to know I'm not a quitter. However, in the matter of my college education, I face no deadlines. There is no wolf at my door saying that I have to finish school in the traditional four years. I'm not even a traditional student. If we have a child I can take some time off, or go part-time. Just so it remains understood between us that I will finish eventually."

"Do you mean it?" Jeremy asked humbly.

"Yes," she said, and all the love she had in her heart was poured into that one word. "Yes and yes and yes. If there's one thing I know, it's that babies are more important than almost anything, and marriages are more important than positions and education and pride and—"

But she was cut off in mid-sentence by the feel of his lips on her eyes, her nose, her chin.

She laughed breathlessly. "I have been so foolish, Jeremy. I have made so many mistakes."

"We have all been foolish, Lindsey. Your parents, mine. You. Me. A bunch of foolish people living their lives the best they knew how."

"Will we make more mistakes, Jeremy?"

"Undoubtedly. But the sum, the total, doesn't have to be a mistake. You and I have taken some big steps. You, when you went to see my father, and I, when I married you."

Their conversation ceased for a while as they lay holding each other, delighting in the new trust that was between them.

"My father made his peace with you today," Jeremy stated. "Now he will be able to go happy through the veil."

"Through the veil," Lindsey murmured. "That's nice, like a gentle passing, a growing."

"Umm."

"But he made more than peace."

"Oh?"

"He made restitution." Smug amusement was in her voice.

"Restitution?" he queried.

"You." She snuggled against his bare chest. "He told me that he owed me a great debt, that he had stolen my family from me. The only restitution he could think of was you."

"You mean I was payment for his debt?"

"Uh-huh. Like a lamb to the slaughter."

"And has the debt been redeemed, my love?"

Lindsey Boulanger reached up and pulled his head down to hers. "Payment has been made—" her hands wandered down the length of his body as her lips fused with his, "—in full."

*   *   *   *   *

WRITTEN IN THE STARS

MAN FROM THE NORTH COUNTRY
by Laurie Paige

What does Cupid have planned for
the Aquarius man? Find out in February in
MAN FROM THE NORTH COUNTRY by
Laurie Paige—the second book in our
WRITTEN IN THE STARS series!

Brittney Chapel tried explaining the sensible
side of marriage to confirmed bachelor
Daniel Montclair, but the gorgeous grizzly bear
of a man from the north country wouldn't
respond to reason. What was a woman to do
with an unruly Aquarian? Tame him!

Spend the most romantic month of the year with
MAN FROM THE NORTH COUNTRY by
Laurie Paige in February. . . only from
Silhouette Romance.

Silhouette Books®

FEBSTAR

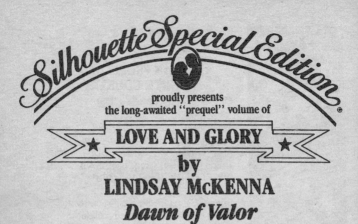

Silhouette Special Edition

proudly presents
the long-awaited "prequel" volume of

★ LOVE AND GLORY ★

by
LINDSAY McKENNA
Dawn of Valor

In the summer of '89, Silhouette Special Edition premiered three novels celebrating America's men and women in uniform: LOVE AND GLORY, by bestselling author Lindsay McKenna. Featured were the proud Trayherns, a military family as bold and patriotic as the American flag—three siblings valiantly battling the threat of dishonor, determined to triumph . . . in love and glory.

Now, discover the roots of the Trayhern brand of courage, as parents Chase and Rachel relive their earliest heartstopping experiences of survival and indomitable love, in

Dawn of Valor, Silhouette Special Edition #649

This month, experience the thrill of LOVE AND GLORY—from the very beginning!

Available at your favorite retail outlet, or order your copy by sending your name, address, zip or postal code, along with a check or money order (please do not send cash) for $2.95, plus 75¢ postage and handling, payable to Silhouette Reader Service to:

In the U.S.
3010 Walden Ave.
P.O. Box 1396
Buffalo, NY 14269-1396

In Canada
P.O. Box 609
Fort Erie, Ontario
L2A 5X3

Please specify book title with your order. Canadian residents add applicable federal and provincial taxes.

Silhouette Books

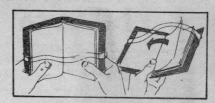

SILHOUETTE·INTIMATE·MOMENTS®

WELCOME TO
FEBRUARY FROLICS!

This month, we've got a special treat in store for you: four terrific books written by four brand-new authors! From sunny California to North Dakota's frozen plains, they'll whisk you away to a world of romance and adventure.

Look for

L.A. HEAT (IM #369) by Rebecca Daniels
AN OFFICER AND A GENTLEMAN (IM #370) by Rachel Lee
HUNTER'S WAY (IM #371) by Justine Davis
DANGEROUS BARGAIN (IM #372) by Kathryn Stewart

They're all part of February Frolics, available now from Silhouette Intimate Moments—where life is exciting and dreams do come true.

FF-1A